A Treasury of Glorious Goddesses

Call Me Ixchel

Mayan Goddess of the Moon

by Janie Havemeyer

Illustrations by Shirin Yim Bridges

 **goosebottom**books

For Julia and Julian.

© 2014 Goosebottom Books LLC

Series editor **Shirin Yim Bridges**

Copy editor **Jennifer Fry**

Typeset in Adobe Caslon Pro and Volkswagen

Illustrations rendered in pen and marker

Photographs unless otherwise indicated are in the public domain, used courtesy of the Creative Commons, or licensed from Shutterstock.

We sincerely thank all contributors to Wikimedia Commons.

Manufactured in the U.S.A.

Library of Congress PCN: 2014931195

ISBN: 978-1-937463-96-0

First Edition 10 9 8 7 6 5 4 3 2 1

Goosebottom Books LLC

543 Trinidad Lane, Foster City, CA 94404

www.goosebottombooks.com

Cast of Characters

Ixchel	Goddess of the Moon
K'inich Ajaw	God of the Sun
Chac	God of Rain and Lightning
Chac Noh Ek	God of the Morning Star (K'inich Ajaw's brother)
Ek Chuah	God of War
Hero Twins	The Demigods, Hunahpu and Xbalanque
Hun Came	Lord of the Underworld
K'awil	God of Corn
Kukulcan	God of the Wind
Manik	God of Human Sacrifice
Vucub Came	Right-hand demon to Hun Came
Vulture King	King of Meavan
Xochipilli	God of Flowers, Music, and Dancing

The Rock Star of Heaven

When K'inich Ajaw, God of the Sun, first spoke to me, he changed my life. He's such a smooth talker. He oozes sparkle and shine. Imagine sitting in a dark arena and suddenly, lights flash and the number-one rock star in the world leaps out of a billowing cloud of dry ice. That's what it's like when K'inich Ajaw appears. However, before he uttered those first words to me, I didn't think about him at all. I was too busy enjoying life as a gorgeous Mayan goddess.

Back then, I was living with my grandfather in the Upperworld, home to the gods and goddesses of the ancient Mayan universe. My grandfather is a worrywart. It's a sure sign he's about to launch into one of his sermons when he starts to pace around and wring his hands. He was always warning me about hanging out with my god friends.

"Gods have dark sides and you don't want to be in their crosshairs when they get angry," he would say.

"What's all the worry about?" I'd ask.

"The universe is a very scary place, Ixchel. You could get hit by a falling star or fall into a thundercloud. If you stay close to home there's less danger something bad will happen."

This might make sense to some people, but not to me. Where's the fun in choosing the safe path? Why not be adventurous and try new things?

After getting my chores done one day, I decided to hang out with Chac, God of Rain and Lightning. Chac unleashes booms of thunder that are so loud I have to cover my ears. His lightning bolts explode and sizzle. He's always up to something exciting.

I found him standing on an outcrop of rock at the edge of the Upperworld, where the sky stretched out before him like an ocean.

He smiled broadly when he spotted me. "Want to help me throw lightning bolts?"

I heard Grandfather's voice in the back of my head, *Don't do it. You might burn your hand or burst your eardrums.*

I reached out for a lightning bolt anyway. There were so many to choose from. I grabbed a grapefruit-sized ball from Chac's arsenal and hurled it down into the sky. There was a fizzle and the bolt split into a tree of light with hundreds of branches going this way and that.

Chac hooted in delight, "Ixchel, you're a natural. I dare you to try the ribbon bolt next."

I wished Grandfather could be more like Chac, encouraging me to try new things instead of saying, *watch out!*

"Hand one over," I said without hesitation.

"Okay, but first I'm going to warn the Mayans with a thunder crack."

Before Chac had the chance to hit a cloud with his thunder axe, Kukulcan, God of the Wind, appeared. Kukulcan and Chac are best friends. They often work together. Kukulcan can fill his cheeks with so much wind that they expand like the belly of a puffer fish.

"Wait," Kukulcan suggested. "If you two are concocting a thunderstorm, let me get some wind going. Then we'll really cause a stir."

Who can resist causing a stir? "We'll wait," I said.

"Okay, my friend," said Chac. "Give us your best breath."

Kukulcan paused to inhale deeply. His brow furrowed and his eyes narrowed. His cheeks began to inflate. His face turned as red as a chili pepper. Just when he looked ready to explode, he exhaled. It made a high-pitched sound like a pack of angry howler monkeys. The wind flattened my clothes and tore at my hair. Meanwhile, Chac's thunderclap was so loud, I had to cover my ears. Then, I grabbed a hot ribbon bolt, bent my arm back as if I were throwing a spear, and yelled,

"Wahooooooo!"

The bolt streaked through the sky like a twig on fire, leaving behind a tingling, scarlet mark on my palm.

"Whoopee!" shouted Chac. "The Mayans will never forget this storm."

"Super Storm Kukulcan," bellowed Kukulcan, trying to high five Chac.

"You mean Super Storm Chac," frowned Chac.

"Come on," I shouted. "Let's do it again."

So we did, until we were so tired and sweaty, we had to plop down on our backs to cool off.

It was then that we all noticed K'inich Ajaw approaching along the western edge of the sky. It was dusk and the skies had cleared.

"Ugh," groaned Chac. "Look who's coming. That guy thinks he's the bee's knees, always gliding by, never stopping to chat with the rest of us. It's as if the world revolves around him."

"Well, it kind of does," Kukulcan replied. "If it weren't for him, Mayans wouldn't be able to grow anything."

Chac just grunted. He doesn't like it when Kukulcan challenges him on things. Besides, it was obvious that Chac was jealous.

The conversation then turned to my latest hairdo. Chac and Kukulcan were always teasing me about my hair. I was especially proud of my hairdos, which I designed myself. This one was a doozy. It was a braid with a living, breathing emerald snake intertwined through the plaits.

"What's with the snake?" asked Kukulcan. "He hisses way too much."

Granted, the snake was a loud accessory, especially when anyone got too close. But I had designed the look with the intention of upstaging all the other goddesses in the Upperworld, and this took some creativity.

It was then that I heard a voice say, "Snappy hairdo!"

I looked around, wondering who was speaking, and realized it was K'inich Ajaw. Before I could acknowledge his compliment, he had already moved on. No wave. No pause for follow-up conversation. Just gone.

"He puts on the charm when he wants something," Chac said in disgust. "Don't you think he's full of himself?"

"Sounds like someone is a bit jealous," Kukulcan teased, which made Chac's scowl deepen. Chac looked over at me, hoping I would agree with him.

If Chac had asked me what I thought of K'inich Ajaw a minute earlier, I might have said the same thing. K'inich Ajaw is very handsome, and since he keeps his distance from the rest of us, it's easy to assume he's arrogant. But at that moment, his compliment made me absurdly happy. I could feel the warm blush on my face.

"I think he is really cute," I said with a grin.

This, of course, made Chac even angrier. He stormed off. Kukulcan and I just rolled our eyes. That's Chac for you, feisty and jealous.

"I think Chac wants to be top dog in the Upperworld!" I said to Kukulcan.

"Of course," replied Kukulcan. "He can be really annoying when he gets competitive."

"I know. He's so predictable that way."

"He's a really good friend though," added Kukulcan. "He always has your back."

"And he's fun."

"Too bad he isn't around to hear all this mushy stuff," chuckled Kukulcan.

"He would eat it up," I agreed. "See you later Kukulcan." It was time for me to head home to Grandfather.

"So long, Ixchel," he replied. "*Kanantabaa*, take care of yourself."

My home was a low-slung stone house with a thatched roof next to the Milky Way. It had a front porch with a sweeping view of the Upperworld. On a clear day, I could even make out the jungles, deserts, and mountains of the Mayan Middleworld far below us. Grandfather and I sat on this porch every afternoon. I would recline in my cozy crescent-shaped throne, which is part hammock, part chair, and give him a recap of my day. Of course, I was always careful to leave out the spicier details.

My version of that day's events went like this:

"I hung out with Chac and Kukulcan today. Chac threw a few lightning bolts down to earth, but don't worry, I stood far enough away so I wouldn't get burned."

"What about Kukulcan? Did he cause any trouble?"

"He blew some wind, but nothing serious," I replied, trying not to laugh at the memory of his bloated cheeks.

"Any other gods or goddesses out and about?" Grandfather asked.

"The sun god passed by," I said.

Grandfather made a face, "He's a hothead. Stay away from him."

Typical Grandfather! He just has to warn me

about everything.

After this conversation, it was a relief to leave the house to do my last chore of the day. It's probably my most important one. I am the moon goddess. Some say it is my beauty that outshines all the other stars in the inky night sky. While this is flattering, the truth is simpler—I light moon torches at twilight. The torches sit in the grooves of a stone ring, like candles on a cake. This stone ring sits close to my home, on a hill. When all the torches are lit, the moon is full. But, I style the moon the way I style my hair. I like to mix things up. I can make the moon look like a fingernail clipping, or a tortilla folded in half. It all depends on how many and which torches I light.

As I considered what shape I wanted to give the moon that night, I thought again about K'inich Ajaw's comment. I couldn't believe he actually noticed my hairdo. It gave me butterflies thinking about it.

Love in Disguise

Grandfather's suspicious nature can overrule his good judgment. I found this out the hard way. After the "snappy hairdo" comment, I designed another hairstyle. This time, I braided my hair and coiled the braids around my head in loops. I stuck glittering green and blue *quetzal* tail feathers into my braids to create a fan-shaped headdress. On the morning I showed off my new look, a hummingbird with a bright red throat hovered outside my window. Grandfather, who never missed much, noticed him too. Of course, he had to give me a warning.

"Don't feed him," he said. "We don't need any more mouths to feed around here."

I just let Grandfather's comment go in one ear and out the other. I wanted to get started on my chores. The sooner I got them done, the sooner I could hang out with my god friends.

Chores can take a while, since my work depends on what the Mayans need from me each day. I might have to help a woman give birth or nurse someone in bad health. Every day, I fill clay jugs with rainwater for their crops, restock my basket of healing potions and work on my back-strap loom, weaving a new *huipil,* or blouse. My huipils are famous throughout the Middle-world. Women study them closely to learn how to weave their own.

On this day, and many more that followed, I had company while I did my chores. The hummingbird flew into my life and then flew away; he appeared and disappeared and appeared again. I followed Grandfather's advice for once and didn't feed him, and yet, he always showed up. It didn't take me long to suspect that something fishy was going on. It's not often that hummingbirds hang out in the Upperworld.

You have to stay on your toes living here. Gods and goddesses change into animals and birds on a dime, and sometimes, they have ulterior motives for donning disguises. The sudden appearance of the hummingbird was a puzzle that I was determined solve.

"Are you just a bird?" I whispered. "Or one of the gods?"

The hummingbird didn't respond or change into anyone else. He just followed me around as if he were my halo. But pretty soon I began to have some strong suspicions that my feathered friend might be the sun god in disguise. Whenever he showed up, so did thunderheads and puffy clouds that blocked the sun. Whenever the sun was out, the hummingbird was never around. The thought that the hummingbird might actually be the sun god made my heart race. I began to count on his appearance every day, and made sure I had my hair done nicely and wore my vanilla-scented perfume.

Unfortunately, Grandfather also noticed

something was up and began to ask a lot more questions.

"Why is that bird hanging around? Are you feeding him? Are you hiding something from me, Ixchel?" he asked.

"No!" I exclaimed, pretending to be offended by his accusations. But, I could tell Grandfather wasn't convinced.

That night, I left a bouquet of tobacco flowers outside my window. Flowers weren't going to cause trouble for anyone, right? It's not like the hummingbird was a dangerous creature, even if he was potentially the most powerful god in the universe. Why not treat him to a little sweet nectar from the star-shaped petals?

The next morning when I woke up, the sun was still just an orange slice at the bottom of the sky. The hummingbird was nowhere to be seen. Looking back on it now, I realize that Grandfather was unusually quiet that morning as he drank his bowl of warm corn gruel called *atole*. He seemed distracted and didn't give out his usual warnings. When I mentioned that I was planning to hang out with Ek Chuah, God of War, all he said was, "Okay."

I should have known something was amiss, because normally, Grandfather would have discouraged me from hanging out with a god like this. If anyone means trouble, it's Ek Chuah. He loves to start fights and to get people fired up. But, since Grandfather seemed to be giving me a free pass to do something fun, I didn't waste a minute analyzing the situation. I fled.

According to Ek Chuah, there was going to be a war in the Middleworld. Wars were only declared after the Mayans studied the stars and the gods gave the signal to begin.

"You know who gave the signal this time?" asked Ek Chuah.

"Who?" I asked.

"Chac Noh Ek. He's K'inich Ajaw's brother," said Ek Chuah. "Do you know him?"

"Isn't he God of the Morning Star? I haven't met him yet, but I'd like to." I'd always wondered what Chac Noh Ek was like, especially because I knew it couldn't have been easy being K'inich Ajaw's brother.

"He's the one," said Ek Chuah. "Do you hear the music? The Mayans are summoning me, too."

"Can I come with you?" I asked. "I've never seen a battle up close."

"Okay," he agreed. "But you're going to have to change into something. I'm going as an eagle."

"I'll go as a quetzal," I said. No point in looking drab.

The Mayans sure did let it rip getting ready to fight. Some beat on giant sea-turtle drums, others blew on conch-shell horns and stone whistles. Their music sounded like a cacophony of moaning sea lions and chirping birds to me, but I could tell Ek Chuah got a kick out of it all. He kept soaring over the crowd.

Next came the battle phase of the war. There

are so many swamps and rain-soaked jungles in the Middleworld that I was surprised the Mayans found enough open space to throw their spears and aim their slingshots. Watching at close range was pretty gruesome. Soldiers got mashed by clubs and pierced by arrows. Honestly, I could have done without all the bloodshed, but Ek Chuah didn't seem to mind.

"That is by far one of the best perks of my job," he confessed when it was all over.

"Don't tell me you like watching people kill one another?" I asked.

"I'm the god of war," he said. "Of course I like it."

But I decided that I wasn't going to watch any more battles up close. My head was pounding and my stomach hurt. I was ready to go home. I needed a strong cup of hot chocolate. I wanted to snuggle with my pet rabbit, maybe even watch the hummingbird do his aerial tricks. I needed to get all those bloody images out of my head.

When I got home, Grandfather was not there. I noticed his blowgun was missing from its hook on the wall and assumed he was out hunting.

In my room, I collapsed onto my bed. I was about to cuddle with my rabbit when I noticed something resting on my windowsill. I slowly got up. A wave of fear coursed through me.

"Oh no!" I said out loud. "Please don't let that be the hummingbird."

The hummingbird was lying on my sill and he was seriously hurt. He had a wound on the side of his chest. I cupped his feathery body in my hands and pressed my ear to his breast. I felt a surge of hope when I heard his heart beating faintly. I knew I had to act swiftly if I wanted to save his life.

I grabbed my basket of healing potions and set to work. I slipped some droplets of tree sap into his beak. His heartbeat picked up. Then I examined his wound. Lo and behold, there was a pellet inside, just like the pellets Grandfather used in his blow-gun. I gently pried it out and dressed the wound with some ointment. By nightfall, I was able to relax. The hummingbird had begun to stir. I tucked him safely inside a small basket and covered him with a lily pad. Then, I sat down to wait for Grandfather to come home.

He finally returned for dinner.

"Did you kill something today?" I blurted out, wondering if he would admit to anything.

"Nope, bad day for hunting," Grandfather replied.

I knew Grandfather wasn't telling the truth. I was sure he had shot the hummingbird. But, instead of feeling angry, I felt secretly triumphant. I had foiled his dastardly plan. I would keep the hummingbird's survival a secret from him. I knew the bird's life depended on it.

At dinner, I shared my usual daily re-cap, relaying the tamer details of my day with Ek Chuah. Grandfather listened quietly. He was not his usual self, bursting with questions and warnings.

"That Ek Chuah is crazy," was all he said.

"I'm going to bed."

It didn't take long before the hummingbird regained his strength. Now, he could come and go as he pleased, but I knew he would always reappear at my windowsill sooner or later. It was as if an invisible string joined us.

Then one night, I was startled awake by a soft rapping on my window. A figure draped in a jaguar cloak peered in at me. Normally, a sight like this would cause alarm, but I didn't feel afraid. I recognized those chocolate brown eyes. I had been expecting K'inich Ajaw for a long time.

K'inich Ajaw crawled through my window and let his cloak fall off. I gasped. He was even more handsome up close. His skin was the color of dark amber. His hair was glossy and black, like obsidian. His arms and legs were muscular and strong. He smelled like the woody smoke of a campfire.

"You were the hummingbird, weren't you?" I asked.

"I couldn't hide myself from you any longer," said K'inich Ajaw. "I've been in love with you for so long."

From that moment on, K'inich Ajaw and I saw each other every day. He came to visit when the Upperworld was dark and quiet and Grandfather was fast asleep. Before dawn, he disappeared. He was even better company now that he had changed back into a god.

"Did you hear what Chac did today?" he whispered in my ear.

"What did he do this time?" I asked, knowing that Chac had a way of getting into trouble.

K'inich Ajaw chuckled, "He got mad at Kukulcan for creating a storm without him. It was a tornado! Now the two aren't speaking to one another."

"Oh Chac," I sighed. "He's so sensitive."

"Hotheaded if you ask me. So NOT cool!" K'inich Ajaw pranced around the room imitating Chac when he got angry. I couldn't help laughing.

K'inich Ajaw plopped next to me on the bed and began to brush my long, black hair. He loved doing that. He also loved playing with my snake and feeding carrots to my rabbit. Often, he tickled me with a long quetzal feather until I begged him to stop. But there were quiet times, too. While I rubbed red cinnabar onto my nails, K'inich Ajaw would munch on squash seeds and watch me.

For a long time, we created a secret little universe all our own in the privacy of my bedroom, right under Grandfather's nose. He didn't suspect a thing.

"We are like two caterpillars," joked K'inich Ajaw. "Tucked away in a cocoon, waiting for the day when we will fly away together."

I found myself paying closer attention to my chores, now that I wasn't always running out of the house in search of a good time. I only wanted to be with K'inich Ajaw anyway, and counted the hours until I would see him again.

"Looks like my granddaughter is growing up.

It's nice to see," Grandfather said to me one day. "Guess I don't need to keep such an eagle eye on you any more."

I couldn't help smiling. I felt pretty clever knowing that I had managed to keep a big secret from him for so long. But, you can't keep a secret hidden forever. It starts to fester. My love for K'inich Ajaw was getting too big to be contained in my little room. Our cocoon began to feel like a prison.

"Let's run away and get married," K'inich Ajaw declared. "Then, we'll have the freedom to do whatever we want together."

"I want to," I said. "But Grandfather is so protective of me. He's never going to let me marry you. Look what he did to you when you were just a hummingbird paying too much attention to me."

"We will escape far away where he can't find us."

"We can't hide forever. We have jobs to do," I said.

"I'll find a way to make it work," he replied.

"How?" I asked, looking him in the eye.

"Trust me," said K'inich Ajaw. "Nothing is impossible if we're together."

After this conversation, I thought about becoming K'inich Ajaw's wife night and day. I wanted to be with him so badly, but I couldn't imagine how Grandfather would ever allow me to marry him. I knew he didn't trust K'inich Ajaw one bit.

Around this time, Grandfather began to get suspicious again. I was easily distracted and he caught me daydreaming. He began snooping into my business and watching me like a hawk. He stayed up at night waiting until I'd returned from my moon duties. When he strapped his blowgun around his waist with a belt, I knew time was running out.

"Let's run away now," urged K'inich Ajaw. "It's the only way we can be together."

"But Grandfather will find me. I know he

will. Then what will happen?"

"We'll run away first and I'll find a place for you to hide. Then, I'll return to bargain with your grandfather. If his choice is either to see you again as my wife or not at all, he will give in. I'll tempt him with a reward if he agrees to let you go."

"What could that possibly be?" I asked.

"I could make him Lord of the Milky Way," he suggested. "Trust me. I'll think of something good."

So that is what I did. I trusted K'inich Ajaw. I was so in love that I agreed to his plan.

K'inich Ajaw worked out all the details, down to anticipating when Grandfather would have his guard down. There was no way he wanted to be shot with a blowgun pellet again. I just waited and prayed, thinking how mad Grandfather was going to be when he discovered I had run off with the sun god.

One Strike and You're Dead

I was killed by a lightning bolt on the day we escaped.

First, there was a deafening boom, then intense pain flared through my body like burning tree bark. My skin prickled as if millions of bees were stinging me all over. My head felt like a rainstorm of boulders was pounding it.

In the blink of an eye, my death spoiled everything. Before running away, I had tried to imagine the worst thing that could happen. I am not usually paranoid, but the hummingbird incident rattled me. Would Grandfather do something really mean again? He might, but I guess that was the risk I chose to take.

Honestly though, not in a million years did I expect to lose my life.

K'inich Ajaw planned the details of our escape so carefully. He secured a cedar canoe with a palm canopy so it wouldn't be obvious who was paddling like mad across the universe. Our escape route would take us through marshy streams where the tall reeds would hide us. And it was timed for when my grandfather would be asleep. I slipped an herb into his stew that night to make sure his sleep was deep. Before we left, K'inich Ajaw had not been able to resist stuffing chili peppers into Grandfather's blowgun.

"Put that in your pipe and blow it, you old geezer," he said triumphantly.

K'inich Ajaw and I planned to paddle to a distant galaxy where I was going to hide. Then, K'inich Ajaw would return to negotiate with Grandfather.

"Can't you do that now?" I asked. "It would be a whole lot easier than running away first."

"I think if you're out of his reach, he won't have much choice but to agree to our plan," K'inich

Ajaw said.

So, we eloped. As we traveled across the Upperworld in our canoe, I remember feeling a mixture of joy, excitement, and anxiety. Would we make it without being spotted? What would Grandfather do when he woke up? But mixed in with this were also feelings of shame for tricking my grandfather. Did he deserve to be abandoned like this? Would I ever see him again? I quickly pushed these concerns aside and focused instead on the bliss of being with K'inich Ajaw.

Just think, I told myself, *from now on you can be with K'inich Ajaw whenever you want. No more hiding or sneaking around behind Grandfather's back.*

Whenever I got especially nervous, all I had to do was look back at him paddling in the stern. He was so handsome steering the canoe across the sky.

I remember the white stars sparkling like a swarm of fireflies. From earth, night looks as black as a raven, but paddling across it, I saw streaks of cobalt blue, violet, indigo, deep plum, and murky green. Sometimes the air felt as warm as a tropical breeze, but then we would hit icy blasts that made me shiver. I watched giant Jupiter rise in the east as the evening star set in the west. Occasionally, meteors hurtled past us. We glided along the still surface of the night, occasionally hitting ripples and bigger waves, until we reached the belt of Orion. That's where our luck ran out.

We both underestimated Grandfather. He had made a secret deal with Chac to look out for me. He'd even given Chac a list of *GODS IXCHEL SHOULD NOT MESS AROUND WITH*. If Chac got wind of any trouble, he was to notify Grandfather immediately, maybe even throw a lightning bolt to scare away those undesirable companions.

You're probably surprised that Grandfather made a deal with Chac. After all, he wasn't too keen on my playing with thunder and lightning and Chac was the god of both. But Chac was loyal and reliable, and that counted for something in Grandfather's book.

Chac had his own motives, too. To be perfectly honest, I knew he liked me a lot more than just as a friend. He always got so hot and bothered when I admired any of the other gods. No surprise then that when Chac saw K'inich Ajaw paddling with me to the outer reaches of the universe, he threw a fit. He hurled a lightning bolt in our direction just as he was supposed to do. Normally, Chac's aim is excellent. But, because of how much he hated K'inich Ajaw and how shocked he was to see us paddling away together, he misfired badly. He struck me right in the back. The lightning bolt shattered me into a million pieces and I disappeared before K'inich Ajaw even had a chance to react.

I had the sensation of sinking, as if I were being sucked into the depths of the ocean, where the water turns from blue to black. The light faded into darkness so that I could no longer see. I fell down, down, down until finally I stopped moving. I floated, as if suspended in a bowl of honey. Then, the darkness began to fade, replaced by a grey twilight. As my eyes adjusted to the light, I realized I was lying on a wide, black road at the foot of an enormous gate. The lower section of this gate was constructed with human skulls layered one on top of the other. Gazing up at the stone arch that formed the top of the gate, I saw inscribed: *XIBALBA*.

Xibalba, the world below the Middleworld, is the place Mayans go after death. The dead descend through caves in the earth along the Black Road that leads to this Underworld. Mortals must journey through Xibalba before they have any chance of reaching Paradise. It is a place of extreme suffering, ruled by nine demons who are frightful to look at, all skeletons or rotting corpses with protruding eyeballs and a stench that makes you want to gag. Grandfather always warned me about them. "It's not called the Land of Fear for nothing," he'd say.

Of course, as an immortal goddess, I would never have to go to Xibalba, so I was very confused when I realized that's where I landed. This was not going to be good. I heard rustling and noticed a figure lurking in the shadows. I couldn't make out his features, but an overpowering smell of rotten chicken hit me. My head hurt badly and I was dying of thirst. I had made a huge mistake by running off in secret with K'inich Ajaw.

Playing Ball With Demons

"Greetings, Ixchel!" said Vucub Came, right-hand demon to the head demon of Xibalba, as he stepped from the shadows. "You look very beautiful today. What brings you down here?"

Vucub was not a pleasant looking fellow. His body was bloated and covered in sores. On his head he wore a wreath made of eyeballs and little bells that jangled when he moved. Seeing him for the first time, you would probably scream and run, or freeze in terror, or throw up. Grandfather had warned me about him too. I tried not to cringe.

"Vucub Came! What a pleasant surprise," I said in my sweetest voice. "My friend Chac just hit me with a lightning bolt."

"Sounds almost as bad as some of the things we do here," chortled Vucub.

"How did I end up in Xibalba?" I asked. "I thought immortals didn't have to pass this way?"

"They don't! You must have accidentally fallen through a rift in the Milky Way. That's the only point of entry from the Upperworld." The way Vucub looked at me made me feel as if spiders were crawling over my skin. "Why did Chac strike you with lightning anyway?"

"Not worth explaining. It's complicated," I replied.

He looked disappointed by my response.

"Maybe you can help me get back, though?" I asked sweetly.

"Well, that's complicated too. You'll have to come with me till we sort it out."

"Where to?" I tried to sound nonchalant.

"The ballcourt," replied Vucub. "Hun Came wants to meet you. I'll escort you."

That didn't sound too terrible. The ballcourt of Xibalba was legendary. Grandfather had taught me all about the Mayan game of *pohatok*. When played on the Middleworld ballcourts, the defeated players didn't just lose the game, they were killed as sacrificial offerings to the gods. The first time Grandfather had explained this, I was shocked.

"That's horrible. Why do they do that?"

"They do it for the overall good of their people," he explained. "It's an honor to be sacrificed, because you're keeping order in the universe."

But on the Xibalban ballcourt, the rules of pohatok changed. The ball game was the first test Mayans had to perform on their journey through the Underworld. They played against demon ballplayers, and if the Mayans won, they could pass straight into Paradise, avoiding the pain of Xibalba. If they lost, they continued on their hazardous journey.

I wanted to see this infamous ballcourt, so I followed Vucub with more curiosity than dread. The Black Road meandered slowly downhill on the other side of the entrance gate. A scruffy looking pack of dogs surrounded us as we walked.

Bats circled overhead and an owl hooted.

"Heh heh," Vucub chortled again. "When you hear the owl hoot, someone is going to die."

What a scumbag, I thought. I tried to stifle his putrid smell by putting my hand over my nose. His little bells jingled and jangled as he trotted ahead like an excited puppy. I couldn't wait to ditch Vucub as soon as possible.

"We're almost there," he gleefully shouted over his shoulder. I could hear faint shrieks in the distance. As we moved closer, I heard louder groans and gasps.

"Welcome to the Xibalba ballcourt," Vucub said as we entered a limestone arena. A crowd of about fifty spectators sat on stone benches watching the game.

"Who are they?" I whispered. "They look like zombies."

"You're right," snickered Vucub. "They're dead Mayans whose turn will soon come to play pohatok against the demons. Until then, they just watch and wait."

The ballcourt of Xibalba didn't look too different from the ones in the Middleworld. It was the size of a modern-day basketball court, and shaped like the capital letter I. Spectators sat opposite one another on stone benches that protruded from the base of the walls running along the playing alley, the narrowest section of the ballcourt. Above the spectators' heads at center court, two stone hoops jutted out of the opposing walls like ears.

Two teams were knocking a rubber ball back and forth in the playing alley. The players were not allowed to touch the ball with their hands or feet, just their hips, body, legs, and arms. The object was to keep the ball aloft on your side of the court without it bouncing, and to send it back to your opponent's side as soon as possible.

I could make out a team of Mayans at one end, and on the opposing side, some of the notorious demons of Xibalba. I spotted Hun Came,

Lord of the Underworld, on a stone throne raised up on a dais where the ballcourt ended at the top of the I. This was called the end zone. He was smoking a cigar. All demons of the Underworld love cigars. It's their signature accessory, the way a warrior always has a weapon.

He waved for us to join him. *Okay, brace yourself,* I thought, and followed Vucub in the direction of the cigar fumes.

"It's good to see you," said Hun, when we approached. "Please, have a seat." He then motioned for us to sit on two stone chairs set on either side of him. "It's a treat for us to have such a beautiful goddess in Xibalba. My demons aren't used to seeing beauty; one can get tired of putrefaction and rot."

"Thank you, Lord Hun." It was in my best interest to be polite. "I've always heard how exciting pohatok is to watch. I'm honored to be here."

Of course, I was lying. Even though I love seeing new things, now that I was in Xibalba, the whole place was giving me the creeps.

Hun chuckled, "This game has been going on forever. Are you familiar with the rules?"

"I know the basics," I replied. "You earn points if the other team misses a shot at the hoop, lets the ball bounce two times without returning it to your side, or lets the ball bounce outside the boundaries of the court."

"Yes, and you win automatically if you get the ball through the hoops," explained Hun.

"That must be really hard to do," I said.

"It pretty much never happens," agreed Hun.

Just then, the crowd erupted in screams and gasps and Hun motioned for me to be quiet and watch.

"The demons have scored the winning point," Vucub whispered in my ear. "You arrived just in time. Wait till you see what happens next," he cackled.

What a low-life, I thought. I knew perfectly well what was coming next. Grandfather had warned me there are nine levels to the Underworld. Each level is filled with one menace after another, like stinging scorpions, pelting rain, and freezing wind. Often, the demons put the Mayans through a test, like in the House of Bats where fierce, knife-nosed bats try to slice your head off like it's a melon on a vine. If you lose your head, the demons hang it in a calabash tree and bury your body beneath the Underworld ballcourt forever.

Now, the pohatok losers were going to be forced to move deeper into the Underworld. A huge moan escaped from the crowd as the demons linked arms and began to walk in a line across the ballcourt toward their victims. The whole place erupted into pandemonium as the terrified losers began to run and dodge, looking for ways to escape, like mice in a maze. But within minutes, they had all been captured, chained together, and dragged out of the arena, heading to a new test or torture. I prayed they would all make it eventually to Paradise.

After the last of the players disappeared from sight, there was a sharp blast from a conch-shell horn.

"What's happening now?" I asked.

"We have a special performance to entertain the spectators while the next group of ballplayers gets ready to play," Hun replied.

A performance. Now this sounded better; although, I was worried that the demons' idea of entertainment was more pain and suffering.

Two dancers wearing scaly armadillo masks swooped into the stadium to the beat of drums. Their feathered headdresses fluttered as they moved. Music from their flutes filled the air. A dog trotted around them, then burst into flames. The crowd gasped; someone screamed. But the next minute, the flames went out and the dog reappeared whole and unscathed.

"Who are they?" I asked.

"They're demigods, the famous Hero Twins," said Hun.

"The two boys who once defeated the demons of Xibalba?" I asked.

"Yes," he confirmed. "They're performing tricks of death and rebirth. It's an especially appealing show to watch when you're dead."

The story of the Hero Twins was legendary. At the beginning of time, when the Mayan universe had just been formed, the twins, Hunahpu and Xbalanque, beat the demons at pohatok, the only humans ever to do so. This feat earned the twins divine status and they were forever known as demigods. They now lived in Paradise. Their story gave ordinary Mayans hope that they would pass safely through Xibalba and reach Paradise, too. I knew I had to find a way to meet these clever demigods as soon as possible. Surely they could help me get out of Xibalba.

The twins performed a few more miracles, like chopping off their heads and reattaching them. As they danced off the stadium floor, the next batch of ballplayers began to suit up.

Ball playing was a dangerous sport. The rubber ball was hard and traveled so fast that it was not uncommon for it to break bones, or skulls. A new group of Mayans was now putting on helmets and heavy cotton padding for protection.

Vucub started to snicker and cackle again. He sounded like a crazy person. "Look at the spectators," he said. "Don't they look terrified they will be called to play next?"

Enough of this, I thought. "If you don't mind," I said to Hun, "I would like to get some fresh air before the next team plays."

"Go on and make yourself at home," said Hun. "But don't miss the next game. I'm sure you'll find it exciting."

"I wouldn't dream of it!" I don't think Hun picked up on my sarcasm.

It was a relief to escape Hun and his awful cigar smoke. I was determined to find those twins and devise a plan to get out of this place.

I eventually found them chatting with the

Demon of Pus, a corpse covered in oozing sores. Meeting Hunahpu and Xbalanque was thrilling. I had heard so much about them and now, they were standing in front of me, even cuter than I had imagined. The twins had long black hair pulled back into ponytails. Tattoos covered their arms and torsos. Hunahpu was dressed simply in a loincloth and a puma cape. Xbalanque wore even more jewelry than I did. I couldn't help but admire his beaded collar, large turquoise belt, and gold bracelets.

Once the Demon of Pus meandered off, I approached them.

"Hunahpu and Xbalanque, I've been looking for you!"

"Ixchel," said Hunahpu. "What a pleasure to meet you."

"Wow, you're even more beautiful in person," said Xbalanque.

"Thank you," I said, stopping to enjoy the compliment. "It's nice to finally meet both of you too, even if it has to be in this frightful place. Why do you come here when you could be in Paradise?"

Xbalanque chuckled, "We like performing our show and the demons always provide a captive audience."

"It's captive, all right," I agreed. "But I need your advice. Can you help me get out of here?"

"That's tricky," said Hunahpu. "Xibalba is like a maze or secret society. There is not a lot of movement in and out without the demons controlling the traffic. You'll need an escort to get out."

"From what I've heard," Xbalanque added, "Hun likes having you here. He'll think of many reasons why an escort isn't available."

"How do you get out?"

"We have an escort."

"Can I tag along when you leave?"

"If it were up to us, sure. But you're still going to have to convince Hun. He makes it seem like you can do what you want, but if he wants here, he'll make it hard for you to get out."

Even though I knew I could charm most people into doing what I wanted, I had a feeling Hun would be a tough nut to crack.

"Could you deliver a message from me to the Upperworld when you get back to Paradise?"

"That, we can do," said Xbalanque.

I pulled Xbalanque close, and whispered in his ear, "Please tell K'inich Ajaw I'm trapped at the ballcourt in Xibalba. I need help getting out."

Xbalanque smiled when he heard this.

"Wow, K'inich Ajaw is the most powerful god in the universe. I'm sure he would be able to help you. We'll get your message to him as soon as possible."

"You guys are great," I said. "Let me know if you ever need a favor from me once I get out of here." I realized I was going to have to be patient, which is never easy for me. "In the meantime, I'm going to try to sweet talk Hun into getting me an escort out of this joint."

"Your charm just might work," said Hunahpu.

"I hope so!" I knew it wasn't going to be pleasant trying to charm a rotting corpse. His smell was enough to suffocate the words right in my mouth.

"Here's a tip," said Xbalanque. "Hun likes compliments, especially about how he's managed to discipline the rest of that ragtag group of demons. He's got Vucub at his beck and call. Vucub will do anything Hun asks."

"So I've noticed," I agreed.

After saying goodbye to the twins, I headed back to Hun's throne platform on the ballcourt. When I sat down next to him, I set my charm power on high. I was taking the twins' advice, and I hoped it would work.

"You've managed to pull together quite an impressive team of ballplayers. It's a wonder they're so athletic since they're mostly bones. How did you do it?"

"They practice 'round the clock."

"Coach Hun," I teased. "How did you get to

be so multitalented?"

Hun smiled a little, "It's not easy working with corpses. Their brains are scrambled."

"But obviously, your brain is still working well. You must be a genius."

"Yes, my IQ has not suffered from decay."

"I bet you're a fabulous ballplayer."

A grin of pleasure crossed Hun's face, "I have been told that! You are a clever observer. I'm so glad you'll be with us for a while."

Oh darn it, I thought. This was not going the way I hoped. Time to try a new tactic.

"You know, I would love to stay, but I can't neglect my goddess duties for too long. Is there anyone who could escort me out? I promise to visit again soon."

"The demons are busy right now, as you can see," said Hun.

"What's Vucub up to?" I asked. "He's not escorting anyone to another level, is he?"

"No, but he has his hands full with a load of

corpses at the entrance gate. There's been another war in the Middeworld with a lot of casualties."

"How about if I join the twins when they're escorted out?"

"They're so popular down here, I've extended their tour. You saw the crowd of spectators we have right now, and more are coming."

"Anyone else come to mind who might escort me out?"

"I'll do it," he said with a gleam in his bulging eyeballs. "But, we're having too much fun for you to think about leaving just yet." He patted my knee with his bony hand.

I could see my efforts would be in vain. He wasn't going to let me leave for a while. I needed to come up with another plan, so I decided to explore beyond the perimeter of the ballcourt.

The ballcourt was located on a flat plain. To the north flowed the River of Pus. To the south coursed the River of Blood. Looking east, I could see the stone buildings of the demons' main city.

That didn't seem to be the way to go. I retraced my steps west, hoping to spot the Black Road that led me here, but it seemed to have disappeared into thin air. When I reached the edge of a swamp buzzing with mosquitoes, I turned back. I wasn't going to find a way to walk out. I plopped down in the shade of a lone ceiba tree, and for a long time, felt too discouraged to get up.

For the next thirteen days, I watched so many rounds of pohatok that I knew I would never watch another game once I regained my freedom. Even watching the demons dragging the next round of losers away lost some of its horror. This began to trouble me. Was I becoming used to all the pain and suffering? Was I going to become the only immortal to get trapped in Xibalba forever? As the days slipped by, my hopes for an escape began to fade. As I fell into despair, something finally happened.

I was taking a break from the ballcourt, sitting under my ceiba tree, remembering all the beautiful things in the universe, when I began to feel dizzy. I lay down and closed my eyes. When I opened them again, I couldn't see a thing. I felt as if I were blindfolded. I had the sensation of falling and then floating. A cold mist settled over me and I shivered. Then, I began to see glimmers of light. I heard wood cracking and splitting, as if a tree were falling in the forest. Next thing I knew, a swarm of dragonflies lifted me into the air. I was buoyed up by their spindly bodies and gossamer wings. The insects, humming in unison, laid me down on a bed of grass. When I looked up, I saw those familiar chocolate brown eyes.

K'inich Ajaw had saved me! I dove into his arms like a bee into honeysuckle. I felt a huge surge of relief and happiness.

"You found me," I sighed, curling my arms around his neck.

"Sorry it took me so long. I got into a brawl with Chac. Nobody messes with my girl without consequences."

"Is Chac okay?" I asked, a bit worried.

"Let's just say he isn't going to play any more tricks on us again soon, but he's fine. A little wounded pride perhaps. I'm so glad you're back," murmured K'inich Ajaw as he nuzzled close to my ear. "You know I would never let you disappear forever."

Little did I realize those words would one day come back to haunt me.

The Morning Star Comes Calling

K'inich Ajaw and I were together at last. But this wasn't the only good news. During the thirteen days that I had been away, K'inich Ajaw had convinced my grandfather to accept our marriage rather than fight us. He didn't have to bribe Grandfather with an impressive title, either. Grandfather was worried he might never see me again if he objected.

"Ixchel is old enough to make her own decisions," Grandfather said. "I don't like that you tricked me and ran off together, but I won't get in your way. If Ixchel wants to marry you, that's her choice."

I couldn't believe my good fortune. Sometimes clouds do have silver linings, and mine was finally being able to marry my true love.

"I think I've died and gone to Heaven," I told K'inich Ajaw who burst into laughter. I just loved the way he doubled over and held his stomach when I made him laugh really hard.

"You'll never have to go to Xibalba again," he promised.

We settled in happily together with just each other for company. K'inich Ajaw built a new house for us not far from my moon ring. It was an easy trek each night to light my torches. The house was small, with just one room for cooking, eating and lounging, and one for sleeping. Its intimacy made it charming and cozy. The best part was outside— a lush garden and orchard provided everything we needed. There were tomatoes, chili peppers, sweet potatoes, herbs, gourd trees to make containers, and agave to provide fiber for weaving. In the orchards, I could pick avocado, pineapple, papaya, and guava.

"It's like our own little world," I marveled.

"Our cocoon," laughed K'inich Ajaw.

K'inich Ajaw spoiled me daily with gifts of jade and turquoise jewelry. He built a hutch for my rabbit that looked like a palace and gathered a bevy of baskets for my snake. He admired all my hairdos, even the ones that didn't work so well.

One day, he came home with the news that his brother Chac Noh Ek, God of the Morning Star, was coming to visit.

"That's exciting," I said. "What's he like?"

"He's very handsome like me; although, he isn't as strong," K'inich Ajaw replied. "He can't light the world like I do. His star isn't even always visible in the sky."

Did I detect a hint of sibling rivalry? Maybe. I'd have to judge for myself once I met Chac Noh Ek in person. Turns out I didn't have long to wait, because he showed up that evening.

K'inich Ajaw was right. Chac Noh Ek was handsome, but not in the rugged way of his brother. Instead, he had delicate features and a slight build. But like my husband, he knew how to say just the right thing to charm a snake out of its basket.

First, he hugged K'inich Ajaw. Think giant ceiba tree next to slender pine. Then, he turned to me and kissed my hand.

"Ixchel, you are even more beautiful than my brother described. What a stunning hairdo. I've never seen a hair accessory quite like that."

"Sssssssssssss," hissed my snake. He knows a compliment when he hears one.

I could tell this last comment bothered K'inich Ajaw, because he put his arm around me and asked me to go make a pot of hot chocolate. When I returned with the drinks, the two had disappeared. There was only a note on the table telling me K'inich Ajaw would be back.

Later that night, I asked him why his brother hadn't stayed around so I could get to know him.

"We had some things to talk about alone," was all he was willing to say.

~~~

When I lived with Grandfather, I was always

trying to do my chores as quickly as possible, so I could go out to play. But now that I was a married goddess, I stopped socializing with other gods. K'inich Ajaw preferred that I stay close to home when I wasn't working. If Grandfather had asked me to do this, I would have been very annoyed, but I didn't mind doing it for K'inich Ajaw. His company felt like enough, just like my stomach feels full after a bowl of atole.

Of course, my best friend Chac and I were no longer on speaking terms anyway. I could have visited Grandfather, but he was still sore about what I did behind his back. I could only take his grumpiness for so long. And I liked weaving on my loom, but this wasn't something I wanted to do all day.

So now, all of a sudden, I found myself welcoming the days when my chores took longer. The best days were ones when I had a lot of contact with the Mayans. I spent more time visiting the sick; although, this reminded me a little too much of Xibalba. I visited women who were about to give birth, mixing herbs to ease labor pains. I helped women weave wavy and diamond designs into blouses that told stories of the gods who watched over them. Weaving huipils was a sacred duty women performed for the gods.

But, to be perfectly honest, overseeing the huipil designs made me think a lot about the gods. I began to realize how much I missed them and how much I needed to be social to feel truly happy. Of course, it was always wonderful when K'inich Ajaw came home—then I pretty much forgot how lonely I felt when he was not there.

A few days after his first visit, Chac Noh Ek showed up again. It was the afternoon and K'inich Ajaw was out lighting the world, of course.

"I'm sorry I didn't stay to get to know you the other night," he said. "That's a beautiful piece of weaving you're working on. May I ask, what are you making?"

"It's going to be a blanket for K'inich Ajaw,"

I replied. "And I am glad you've returned."

"So am I," said Chac Noh Ek. "K'inich Ajaw has always been very possessive. He would never let me touch or borrow his stuff. He wanted to talk to me all by himself the other night. We had some catching up to do. But now that you're my sister-in-law, I think I should get to know you too."

"I was surprised that he wanted to keep you all to himself. But I know how stubborn K'inich Ajaw can be. It's hard to change his mind when he's set on something. He can be persuasive, too."

"That's an understatement," chuckled Chac Noh Ek. "When we were boys, he convinced me to mix a fistful of ground-up chili peppers into my hot chocolate so I could breathe fire. But all it did was set fire to my mouth."

I laughed at the idea of flames coming out of Chac Noh Ek's mouth.

"Did you know he convinced me to run away in the middle of the night?" I laughed. "I got hit by lightning during our escape and was trapped in

Xibalba awhile, but it all worked out in the end."

"I heard. He told me all about it and how he wooed you as a hummingbird. He said you are a gifted healer and nursed him back to health."

I blushed remembering it all.

It felt wonderful to have Chac Noh Ek's company as I sat at my loom. We talked for a long time that day about his childhood under the shadow of KJ, which is what he called his older brother.

"It took me awhile to find my place in the Upperworld," explained Chac Noh Ek. "I'm the Morning Star, and KJ often blocks the Mayan's view of me. I'm always there in the mornings, but not always visible. Funny enough, this has made me more important."

"How so?" I asked.

"I became the star that signaled when it was time for Mayans to go to war. When I'm invisible, Mayans wait. When they see me, they consider it the right time to fight."

"That's fantastic," I replied. "What a great way

to step out of your brother's shadow."

When it was time for Chac Noh Ek to go, I felt a little sad, but he promised to return soon and tell me more.

I was so excited by this visit that I couldn't wait to tell K'inich Ajaw all about it. So I was totally unprepared for his reaction. I expected him to be happy. But that is not at all what happened.

"He needs to mind his own business and stop snooping around when I am not at home," K'inich Ajaw said.

"K'inich Ajaw," I replied. "That is ridiculous. I enjoyed his company. He wasn't snooping around. He just told me wonderful things about you, and I enjoyed hearing them."

This seemed to take the wind out of K'inich Ajaw's sails. He smiled then and asked me what wonderful things his brother had said about him. So I told him. Why do gods always change into gentle doves when you flatter them?

Pretty soon, K'inich Ajaw was in a happy

mood again and we spent the evening laughing about how he and Chac Noh Ek got into trouble as boys and how K'inich Ajaw could always wrestle his brother to the ground in the time it takes a monkey to climb a ceiba tree.

"Did you know I once persuaded him to drink hot chili peppers?" K'inich Ajaw laughed. "He flew around like a bumblebee afterwards."

"How could you?" I teased.

But, after this conversation, I stopped telling K'inich Ajaw about his brother's visits, especially because Chac Noh Ek became a regular guest. He usually showed up while I was weaving in the afternoon. He was good company and we became friends. His visits reminded me of the times I had spent with Chac. Both were fun to hang out with; although, Chac Noh Ek was charming, whereas Chac was rough-and-tumble. I missed Chac.

Meanwhile, small things began to change between K'inich Ajaw and me. It started when he wanted to know how I was spending my days. He wanted to know the details, just like Grandfather had. Then, his questions multiplied and he started to ask them the minute he got home.

"What did you do today?"

"Nothing new. My chores. My weaving. Just the same old stuff."

"What stuff?" persisted K'inich Ajaw.

"You know. Helping women weave, making sure babies make it safely out of the womb, visiting the sick."

K'inich Ajaw would look at me as if I had more to "confess." So then, I would try to think of something funny to say.

"I was called to the bed of a sick woman. I know the demon of jaundice is coming for her soon, because her skin is turning yellow. Her husband calls her a bitter old lemon."

All right, I admit, it's a corny, mean joke, but getting the third degree from K'inich Ajaw all the time made me uncomfortable. He used to always laugh at my jokes, but now, he had stopped laughing.

I asked Chac Noh Ek about it.

"What's bugging him?"

"K'inich Ajaw holds things in," said Chac Noh Ek. "But then, they often burst out, like a volcano. You'll find out what's wrong soon enough."

The questions kept coming.

"I heard from Manik that my brother has been stopping by to see you quite a bit. Is that true?"

"What's the god of human sacrifice doing putting his nose in my business? Is he spying on me?"

"Ixchel, answer my question."

"Sure, I've been hanging out with Chac Noh Ek. What's wrong with that? He's your brother."

"I don't want him here when I'm not."

"K'inich Ajaw," I said. "Don't be ridiculous. We're just friends. Don't you want me to be friends with your brother? Now answer my question about Manik. Is he spying on me?"

"Manik tells me what goes on in the Upperworld because I asked him to keep an eye on things while I am busy. Besides, I ought to know. I'm your husband."

"Does that give you the right to tell me whom I can hang out with?"

"You're encouraging my brother to hang out with you!"

"No I am not. He is coming of his own free will. What's wrong with that?"

"Stop seeing him, Ixchel! You are married to me and I want you to stop," he shouted, and then he stormed off.

After this latest argument, I did make a point of asking Chak Noh Ek not to come around when I was alone. He understood. For a while, things calmed down at home.

But I was no longer myself around K'inich Ajaw. I guarded what I said and kept more of my feelings inside. We still laughed and joked around. He still combed my hair and held my hand. But it felt as if his false accusations had created fractures in our relationship. I was afraid that one day, the earth would really quake beneath my feet.

One afternoon, Chac Noh Ek couldn't resist coming to tell me about a war he had averted, just by hiding a few minutes until the Mayans had calmed down. I was happy to see him again, but in the back of my mind, I kept remembering what K'inich Ajaw had asked me to do. I decided to ignore K'inich Ajaw's jealousy and invite Chac Noh Ek to come in.

"Have you finished the blanket?" he asked.

"I have," I said. "It's rolled up and hidden in the rafters of our bedroom. I'm waiting for the right time to give it to him."

"Can I see it?" asked Chac Noh Ek.

How could I deny that request? The blanket had taken me a long time to weave and I was very proud of it. I knew K'inich Ajaw wouldn't approve of his brother seeing his gift first but I was not about to tell him.

"Follow me," I whispered to Chac Noh Ek.

"But don't tell a soul you saw this first." I pulled the blanket out from its hiding place and unrolled it.

"It's beautiful, Ixchel, just like you. K'inich Ajaw is very lucky."

I felt like crying when he said that. It felt wonderful to be appreciated. Deep down, I longed for K'inich Ajaw to tell me he loved me no matter how I spent my free time.

"I'm going to give it to K'inich Ajaw tonight," I said, deciding as I said it. "There's no reason to wait any longer."

"He'll love it," said Chac Noh Ek. He knew just what to say to make me feel better. When he left, he promised to return when K'inich Ajaw was home.

That night, I put on a beautiful jade pendant K'inich Ajaw had given me when we were first married and styled my hair in a creative twist. I set the table with our best mats and put out gourds of tamales, papayas, squash, and honey. I filled a ceramic jug with intoxicating *balché*. I had been soaking balché tree bark and roots in water and honey for days, and now, it was just right. I lit two sticks of incense that made our house smell of citrus and pine. I sat down and rubbed red cinnabar on my nails. I prayed that K'inich Ajaw would have the same reaction to the blanket that his brother had.

Then I waited.

And waited.

And waited.

K'inich Ajaw didn't come home for dinner that night.

The incense burned down until it died. The food sat untouched in the gourds. The sky faded to grey, then to coal black. I fell asleep in my chair.

I woke up to screaming.

"You let him in again! I told you not to do that! You let him into our bedroom. What did you do with my brother?"

When I looked up at K'inich Ajaw, his eyes were as crazy as a rabid dog's. Words roared out of his mouth with such force and speed it was impossible to answer. The volcano had erupted, just as Chac Noh Ek had warned.

"Answer me!" K'inich Ajaw shouted.

But when I tried to speak, K'inich Ajaw started shouting again.

"I can't trust you. I should never have plucked you out of Xibalba. You're making my life miserable!"

Then, he started pounding his fist on the table. He grabbed one of the gourds and smashed it onto the ground. Tamales went splat all over the floor. He knocked the bench over.

I knew there was nothing I could say or do to calm him down. K'inich Ajaw was a fire that needed to burn through before dying out. I sat very still in my chair.

"You said you would not see my brother again!" he hollered. "You betrayed me."

He was pacing back and forth now.

"Please listen," I pleaded.

"I don't want to hear any more of your lies!" K'inich Ajaw screamed. "Do you understand?"

He bent over and cried out like a wounded animal. The next thing I knew, he was rushing at me. He swooped me up like a big ocean wave, rolling me into his arms and out the door. Then he threw me right out of Heaven.

I dropped like a feather through the thirteen layers of the Upperworld. I couldn't do anything to stop my descent. Patterns of colors whirred by me as I fell.

Down.

Down.

Down to the Middleworld, where mountain peaks poked through the canopy of clouds like mushrooms in a forest. I finally landed by the rocky banks of a big lake; washed up like debris from a boat wreck.

I lay there for a long time and didn't move. I was in a state of shock. K'inich Ajaw had become someone different. I started to cry. I didn't stop for a very long time.

Under the Wing of a Vulture

The sound of flapping wings startled me into looking up. An enormous black-and-white vulture, about four times my size, had just landed by my feet. Vultures often get a bad rap because they eat the rotting corpses of animals, but they carry messages between humans and gods, so we like having them around. I was so startled by the size of this one that I stopped crying. I glanced quickly around and recognized Lake Atilan in front of me. I was now squarely in the Middleworld. I wasn't happy to be there; although, it was a beautiful spot. Vines of purple flowers snaked around boulders that lined the shore. Three volcanoes rose up along the edge of the lake.

The vulture cooed softly at me. I prayed he didn't mean any harm. His piercing straw-colored

eyes seemed to say, don't be afraid. But I was grip-
ped by panic when he picked me up in his hooked
white bill and plopped me right onto his back.
Then, his great big wings began to flap. I grabbed
on tightly to his feathers and lay as flat as I could
on his back. My heart raced. I tried to breathe
deeply and relax, but I was worried about falling off.
I held on tightly to his feathers as we rose gently
up into the air, gliding over the lake. The water was
so clear I could see all the way to the bottom. We
soared over forests of pine and oak, rising higher
and higher, until soon, we were far above the trees
and grazing the clouds.

The vulture carried me north toward a tall
mountain. As we approached its craggy summit,
he descended slowly, until we skimmed the stone
ramparts of a huge acropolis.

From my downy perch, I saw that the city
had been built on top of a mountain, where it
leveled off into a flat plain. Paths connected large
limestone buildings to one another. Small orchards

and gardens were sprinkled throughout. A huge wall surrounded the entire city. We circled overhead a few times, sinking lower and lower, until I could make out the faces of people walking around the bustling acropolis. Finally, the vulture headed for a large rectangular plaza at the northern edge of the city. A towering pyramid with a temple on top loomed at one end of the plaza. The largest building in the entire acropolis faced us at the other. The vulture landed softly in front of a tall figure with a feathered headdress. I was still hanging on for dear life. I didn't dare let go yet. The drop from his back to the ground looked steep. The vulture gently lifted me in his bill again and placed me on the ground himself.

I could now see the figure up close and he startled me. He had the body of a man and black hair that he wore in a ponytail. But his large, pendulous nose looked just like a bird's beak. He wore a puma cape, a loincloth, and a fan-shaped gold and turquoise necklace. He looked like a king or a priest.

It wasn't until he bent down to greet me (he was over seven feet tall!) that I noticed his wings. They were hidden discreetly in the folds of his puma cape. At first glance, it was hard to tell what they were. But later, I had a chance to see them outspread. They were green and leathery and as wide as boat sails.

As I was taking stock of my new situation, the creature smiled and said, "Welcome Moon Goddess! I am the Vulture King. I heard you'd been stranded, so I sent my VIP carrier to rescue you. I hope he didn't frighten you?"

For a moment, I had no idea what to say. Was this king a man, a bird, or both? I took a deep breath to compose myself.

"It was kind of you to rescue me. Your vulture gave me a comfortable ride. His size is intimidating but I am grateful for your help. Where am I?"

"You are in my kingdom, Meavan. Vultures, like the one that flew you here, are our carriers.

They come in various sizes, and this one is by far the largest."

"I haven't heard of Meavan," I said.

"Most people don't know about us because we're tucked away on this mountain peak far removed from other Mayan kingdoms. We live a peaceful life here, since we're never attacked."

"How fortunate you are to live here," I said. "I feel lucky you rescued me."

"I've heard so much about you. Your beauty, your work, and your tapestry designs are legendary. It's my honor to have you here."

I didn't feel very beautiful at that point. Let's just say my unexpected journey had wreaked havoc on my hair and clothes.

"I'm inviting you to be my guest in Meavan," continued the Vulture King. "I have even prepared a room for you in my palace."

Frankly, I didn't see what choice I had. But the Vulture King seemed kind and genuine. He was offering me a place to rest. I needed that. Besides, his spread looked pretty impressive from the air. It wouldn't be a bad place to recover. So I said, "Yes, thank you for the invitation."

Two servants led me up a set of marble stairs and into the palace. We walked through a maze of corridors until we came to a bedroom. It was large, with an impressive view over the entire acropolis. Tapestries covered the walls, each one showing a vulture in flight. Looking up at the ceiling was like looking into the night sky because it was dotted with yellow stars on a blue background.

"This is very nice," I said. Then, I was so exhausted that I climbed right onto the big bed in the center of the room and nestled my head into a plush pillow. A servant pulled the bed curtains closed around me. A huge wave of relief washed over me. I had a place to rest and think in private.

None of the things that had recently happened to me made any sense. I'd lost everything that mattered to me. I'd been accused of something I didn't do. What was I supposed to do now?

How could I go on without K'inich Ajaw? Would he change his mind and look for me? Did I even want him to? Could I carry out my duties as the Moon Goddess now that I wasn't in the Upperworld? Where would I go if I went back? Living with Grandfather again would not be easy.

I didn't know the answers to any of these questions. My heart felt like a raw, oozing wound that might never heal. If I slept, at least I could forget all the awful things that had happened to me for a few hours. Then, when I woke up, I could try to get through another day. *One day at a time,* I told myself. *One day at a time.*

I stayed in that bed for days while servants brought me plates of avocado, guava, and papaya, and slices of cornbread. I didn't eat any of it. I sobbed and cried instead. I missed K'inich Ajaw. But as the days passed, my grief over losing him slowly began to dull. I began to ask myself new questions. How could he accuse me of something I didn't do? I loved him. Wasn't that obvious? How dare he throw me out of Heaven? I wasn't some piece of pottery you could toss out the door.

The more I thought about the situation, the angrier I felt. I gave up everything, including my life, to be with him. The real traitor here was K'inich Ajaw. I didn't do anything wrong, he did. Love shouldn't stab you in the heart like a stingray.

One morning, when I woke up feeling angry all over again, I decided I wasn't going to waste one minute more in bed. The Vulture King had been sending me daily messages of concern, suggesting things I might like to do to cheer me up. So, I made the decision to do one of them.

I took a long soak in one of the palace baths; three pools at different temperatures in a dimly lit room. The cold bath jolted me awake while the hot bath soothed and relaxed me. I dabbed perfume on my body and styled my hair. I brushed and braided it into an intricate coil that rested at the nape of my neck. I stuck some black and white vulture feathers into the coil. They weren't quite as impressive as the green snake that I had lost when I left the Upperworld, but good enough. Then, I set out to explore the palace.

I discovered that the Vulture King had an impressive home. I wandered through many rooms. Some were public rooms where citizens of the acropolis gathered and mingled, while others were private rooms for sleeping. There were baths, workshops for weaving, masonry, and ceramics, and temples for praying to ancestors and to gods and goddesses like myself. The biggest room was the throne room where the Vulture King settled disputes and made decisions. His throne was a massive stone bench and his subjects had to crane their necks to look up at him.

The corridors were filled with servants. They carried fruits and vegetables from the gardens and orchards into the kitchen. They barbecued poultry and pounded maize kernels into cornmeal.

The citizens of Meavan began to notice me after I emerged from my bedroom. Pretty soon, word got around the acropolis that there was a goddess in the palace. I began to receive invitations. I was asked to teach weaving and to be present at babies' births. I started to feel a little better.

People heard that I had been sick. They had not seen the moon in a while. Only the stars were left to light up the night. Mayans were praying for me, and knowing this made me feel less alone. It felt good to immerse myself in weaving and birthing, but I missed lighting the night. I was resigned to losing my clothes and jewelry, but I minded very much not having my pets and my torches.

The Vulture King invited me for tortillas with honey and chocolate in his private rooms. We took long walks together in his orchards and gardens. We did a lot of talking. I told him about all that had happened to me with K'inich Ajaw, my grandfather, Chac, and Chac Noh Ek. He was a sympathetic listener.

"Be careful to whom you give your trust," he

said. "You're so charming and fun. It's natural that gods flock to you. But be selective. You want friends who appreciate your qualities of compassion and kindness. All my life people have judged me by my looks," continued the king.

"That must be very hard," I said.

"It hasn't been easy growing up with huge webby wings and a beak," he said. "I've had to earn my people's love and admiration the hard way."

I thought about this awhile. It was true that the Vulture King looked intimidating, especially with his wings unfolded to fourteen feet, but I could see he was well loved by his subjects and that he loved them in return. I couldn't help thinking about how the other gods and goddesses of the Upperworld viewed K'inich Ajaw as arrogant and hot-tempered.

On one of my visits to the king, he surprised me with a wonderful gift. He gave me my clay jugs, healing baskets, and torches. "How did you find them?" I asked, rushing to touch them all again.

"I sent the vulture who rescued you back to the lake to see if K'inich Ajaw had thrown any of your possessions away. He found these scattered around the lake and brought them back to Meavan."

"This is the best gift," I cried. "How can I ever thank you?"

"You don't need to thank me. Just continue your work helping others."

Finally, I had everything I needed to do that. However, fear of running into K'inich Ajaw in the Upperworld prevented me from lighting the night. The world would have to live without moonlight for a little while longer.

I began to establish my routine in Meavan. This felt comforting. I would wake up around dawn and eat *sak'ha*, a corn and honey gruel, for breakfast. Then, I would wander into the acropolis to see if anyone needed help. After lunch, I would usually hang out in the throne room with the king or spend time weaving in a workshop. I was able to weave some new outfits. Then I would bathe, put on a new blouse and skirt, style my hair, and eat dinner with the king in his courtyard. Dinners were delicious—stews flavored with iguana eggs, tamales in chili pepper sauces. Cups of balché and *kakaoh*, a spicy chocolate drink, were always on hand. Afterward, I would play board games with the king while we munched on squash seeds and listened to flute music. When I returned to my room at night, I often found a small gift on my pillow; a turquoise ring or a pair of gold earrings. There was never a note about who had left these gifts, but the Vulture King always smiled when he saw me wearing them.

One evening, I found a scroll of tree bark at my door. It said:

> *The Vulture King requests your presence as*
> *his honored guest at a festival dedicated to*
> *God Xochipilli tomorrow night.*
> *Time: Dusk.*
> *Location: the Plaza.*

I could not believe it. There was going to be a party! I loved parties. For the first time in a long while I felt excited. How should I do my hair? Which one of the king's gifts should I wear? Where could I get my hands on a necklace and a new dress? I thought about these details for the rest of the night. The invitation had encouraged the old me to poke her head out.

The next morning, there was a light rapping on my door. When I opened it, a servant handed me a basket. When I looked inside, I saw a new rainbow-colored huipil and a rope of jade beads. I couldn't wait to try them on. The Vulture King must have read my thoughts, giving me just what I needed without me having to ask. Now I could look my best seated by his side at the festival that night. I put on my new outfit and my latest pair of gold earrings and twirled around in circles in my room.

"Watch out world!" I shouted out loud. No one heard me of course, but it felt fun to shout.

Images of jaw-dropping hairdos started forming in my mind.

The party turned out to be fabulous. It lived up to all my expectations. Xochipilli was God of Flowers, Music, and Dancing, and the citizens of Meavan put on a good show for his benefit. Dancers slithered like snakes to the sound of drums, flutes, and rattles. Servants grilled iguanas and chickens on spits over roaring fires. Flowers in giant urns gave off a sweet aroma. I sat next to the king on a low platform. He made sure my cup of balché was always full.

Many times, I caught him gazing at me. "I have never seen quite such a magnificent hairdo," he whispered.

"Thank you," I said, patting my coiled updo. His gift of jade beads was twisted through my hair and hung down my back like a jungle vine. "You have a pretty spectacular pair of wings yourself."

He gave a hearty laugh then and stood up, which made his wings flap and billow. The musicians stopped playing and the dancers stopped moving. Conversation among the crowd petered out and it became eerily silent.

"Tonight," announced the king, "I am very honored to have a special guest at our festival, the moon goddess, Ixchel. It has been my pleasure to have her company for some time. I hope that she will consider staying with me forever in Meavan."

The Vulture King took my hand and pulled me to my feet. He then surprised me by bending over and pecking me on the cheek. The crowd roared and hooted. The dancers began to twirl. The musicians beat on their drums and shook their rattles. The king smiled and folded his wings before sitting down again.

"That's a wonderful invitation," I said, sitting back down next to him. I even blushed a little. What the king lacked in the looks department, he more than made up for in charm.

"I mean it," he said. "I want you to be happy

and I think you can be happy here."

That night in bed I thought about the king's proposal. He treated me with more kindness than anyone ever had. When I made a mental list of all of his positive qualities, there were many. He was even-tempered, gentle, generous, and kind. He was the best listener. He understood and appreciated me. Most importantly, I knew I could be myself around him. He enjoyed seeing me laughing and talking with others.

I thought about the time I wept on the shores of Lake Atilan. I thought I'd lost everything. Strangely, things were turning out okay; although, I felt sad that I wasn't living in the Upperworld. It was my home and goddesses belong there. But, as long as K'inich Ajaw was there, I didn't want to return. I still thought a lot about him and I was angry at the way he had treated me. I felt a twinge of pleasure thinking about how jealous he'd be if he found out what had happened to me.

The fact was that the Vulture King treated me

with respect and kindness. K'inich Ajaw tossed me out of our home and the Vulture King offered me a new one. The sooner I forgot about K'inich Ajaw, the better. I decided if I could figure out a way to light the night, the reasons to stay far outnumbered the reasons to leave. With time and distance, I hoped the memory of my relationship with K'inich Ajaw would fade away like a bruise. I was all set to tell the king of my decision when I became distracted.

Have you ever felt as if someone were watching you? It's a funny feeling. You walk down the street and sense someone might be following you. But when you turn around, there is no one there. Then you wonder, is my imagination playing tricks on me? Is someone really there or not?

I started to get this feeling of being followed just as the palace was beginning to feel like home. I was well known throughout the kingdom by then, so whenever I emerged from the palace, people stopped to chat with me, to admire my hair, to ask for advice. While engaged in conversation, out of the corner of my eye I would often spot some darting shape or shadow. Sometimes, I thought I saw a deer running by. I told myself, *that's ridiculous. Deer don't live in Meavan.*

I didn't say anything to the king, because I knew he would worry. Instead, I kept vigilant and looked over my shoulder as I walked. I peeked out of my bedroom window when the curtains were drawn. I wedged a large chair against my door, in case someone tried to creep in during the night. Sometimes, I thought I heard a door close or feet scurrying away. Still I saw nothing.

The king, being very sensitive, noticed something was bothering me.

"Is everything okay, Ixchel?" he asked with concern.

"Of course," I said, not wanting to alarm him. "You have provided every creature comfort a goddess could want."

"That's good," he said. "But, you have been

looking a bit tense lately."

"It's nothing," I said. "I'm just thinking about all the new twists and turns my life has taken."

"Let's play some board games," he suggested. "That always makes us laugh."

I smiled. He knew how to cheer me up.

The balché we drank that night made me let my guard down. Once back in my room, I forgot to lock my door. I slipped into bed and pulled the curtains closed. That's when it happened.

If you haven't already guessed it, someone all too familiar came back into my life.

Honey-Moon

K'inich Ajaw's face poked through the folds of my bed curtains like a lizard from a hole. I let out a little gasp. Then, I felt a burst of anger. I wanted to kick him in the gut and shout, *go away you creep!* I also felt like throwing my arms around his neck and kissing him.

"What do you think you're doing sneaking up on me like this?" I shouted. "Don't you dare come near me!"

K'inich Ajaw just tore the curtains apart and pounced onto the bed. I scuttled back like a spider into one corner.

"Answer me!" I barked. "What are you doing here?"

"Ixchel," he stammered. "I've been in agony without you. Ever since you left, I've been trying to find you."

"What do you mean I left?" I snapped. "I didn't walk out on my own. You threw me out!"

"I know. I did a terrible thing. I was so angry. I wasn't thinking straight." K'inich Ajaw spoke in a hushed voice, like someone who felt truly ashamed of his behavior. "I am so sorry, Ixchel, for what I did to you. Can you ever forgive me?" he pleaded.

"No! That was no way to treat someone."

"I was wrong," admitted K'inich Ajaw, who no longer looked like the handsome and confident god I remembered. His hair was disheveled and he had dark circles under his eyes. It certainly looked like he had learned a lesson.

"How did you find me?" I asked, my voice softening.

"I heard rumors you were living with the Vulture King," he said. "It took me a while to track this place down, but I was determined to find you again. I've missed you so much. I need you by my side."

These were surprising words coming from K'inich Ajaw. Maybe he truly had changed.

"I know we were meant to be together," he continued. "We are two sides of the same coin—the sun and the moon. I won't ever hurt you again. I promise."

I really wanted to believe what K'inich Ajaw was telling me. But could I trust him again? Now that he was sitting right next to me, I knew that I loved him as deeply and passionately as I always had. But I didn't dare tell him this yet.

"You hurt me badly, K'inich Ajaw," I said. "It's going to take more than an apology to get me back."

"What is it going to take?" he asked.

"The Vulture King treats me really well. I know you are still my husband, but he wants me to stay here. He respects me."

"You belong with me," K'inich Ajaw exclaimed. "We need to be together. You belong in the Upperworld."

"K'inich Ajaw, you don't understand," I scolded. "I need to think about what is best for me. If you can prove to me that you've really changed, I might consider giving you another chance. But I am not packing my bags tonight."

"I will prove to you that I've changed," he declared, his old confidence resurfacing. "This half-man-half-bird king you've been hanging out with can never love you the way I do."

K'inich Ajaw sat up straight and puffed out his chest.

"Sweet words, K'inich Ajaw. But the proof will not be in words but in your actions," I said. "You'd better leave now. You scared me by creeping up on me. Next time, you should think of a better way to get my attention."

"Of course. Whatever you want," he said, as he slid off my bed.

Then he stood up tall and gazed down at me with that familiar look in his eye, "You look beautiful. It's good to see you again."

"Think carefully about what I said," I warned, refraining from showing him how good it was to see him again too. Better to play it cool and see if he really was a changed person.

He pulled my bed curtains closed and disappeared into the night.

I didn't see K'inich Ajaw again for a while, but he left signs that he was thinking about me every day. Bouquets of plumeria and water lily, a pouch of cacao beans, and an eagle-feather head-band were left on my windowsill, with notes like *I love you* or *IX&KJ forever*. He wrote poems about love, destiny, and forgiveness. And he became super creative in showing his adoration—sunsets became so beautiful that even the Mayans began to wonder what was going on. Slowly, over time, his efforts had an effect. His gestures of love won me over; especially the sunsets. I convinced myself that it was worth giving K'inich Ajaw a second chance.

But first, I needed to speak with the Vulture

King. One night, while we were eating dinner, I screwed up my courage to tell him the whole story.

"I had an unexpected visitor not too long ago," I began. "My husband, K'inich Ajaw. He found me at last."

The Vulture King looked startled. "Are you okay?" he asked.

"Yes, he was very well behaved," I assured him. "K'inich Ajaw wants me to come back to him. He is still my husband and I think he's really changed since I've been gone."

The king hung his head so I couldn't see the expression in his eyes. "What do you want to do?" he asked.

"I want to give him a second chance," I blurted out. "I still love him."

"Love is a powerful emotion," said the king. "I have felt it deeply, too."

He looked up and I could see that his eyes were swimming with tears. "I can't stop you from doing what you want, but I will worry about you."

I placed my hand over his. "You have been kinder to me than anyone has ever been. I will never forget you. But I can't stay here if I am still in love with my husband."

"I want to beg you to stay with me because I'm in love with you, too." The king cast his eyes down bashfully when he said this. It was the first time he told me this; although, I had known it for a long time.

"I love you too," I said. "In the way you love a friend."

"I know you do," said the king. "Anyway, this is not about how much I love you. It's about you. Do you really think K'inich Ajaw has changed?"

"Yes," I answered, more certain than I felt. "If he were still the same god and knew that I was now with you, his jealousy would have kept him from asking me to come back."

"I can't stop you from going back to him," repeated the Vulture King. "But I'm not going to pretend to like it."

"You will always be my friend," I said. "You rescued me when I really needed help. I will never forget that. But I am a goddess, after all. I should live in the Upperworld. One day, you will find a companion who is just right for you."

The Vulture King sighed. "There aren't too many people like me in this world."

That night, I began to pack the beautiful jewels and clothing the king had given me during my stay in Meavan. As I placed the last pair of earrings in a pouch, my heart began racing so much that I had to sit down on the edge of the bed. I knew I was taking a big gamble going back to K'inich Ajaw. It was hard to know for certain whether he had truly changed. All I knew was that our love was real and that I wanted to believe things would be different.

To help calm my fears, I decided I needed to ask K'inich Ajaw some more questions before returning home with him. I sent an owl messenger to find him and he came right away. He broke into a huge smile when he saw all the bulging pouches I had packed in my room.

"Stop smiling," I teased. "I only travel light when I leave unexpectedly." Then I got very serious. "I'm thinking of coming home, but you have to promise me a few things."

K'inich Ajaw looked like a dog that was about to be given a special treat. He sat up really straight and opened his eyes wide. "I'll do anything you ask," the words spilled out of his mouth in a rush.

"Hold on and wait to hear what I have to say," I warned.

"Rule number one: you cannot expect me to stay in the house all day and not talk to anyone else. Rule number two: there is no need to feel jealous of anyone else. You have to trust me. Rule number three: no more throwing things around the house. Go cool off somewhere else when you get mad. If you can promise to do all these things, we can be together again."

K'inich Ajaw beamed. "Of course I agree. I

will do all those things and more. I will cherish you and be as helpful as I can around the house. You will see. I've changed. You won't regret coming home."

"Okay, so you promise?" I needed to make sure he heard me. "Tell me what you need to do."

K'inich Ajaw recited all the rules exactly as I had said them.

Then, for good measure, I added, "If you forget any of these rules, I'm not staying. I have an open invitation to return here at any time."

K'inich Ajaw looked at me like a sad puppy and frowned.

"Okay," I sighed. I found it so hard to resist him when he looked that way. His reassurances had helped calm my fears. "You now have my permission to sweep me off my feet."

K'inich Ajaw didn't waste a second picking me up in his arms again. He hugged me close and I could feel the heat of his skin and his warm breath. He swooped me back up to Heaven, my pouches flying behind us like a flock of swallows.

Our house looked just the same as when I had left it, but of course, all the broken crockery and food had been cleaned up. There were tobacco flowers on the table. My rabbit crouched inside his little palace munching leaves. I rushed over to pick up my snake who lay curled in his basket.

K'inich Ajaw lit some *copal* incense.

"I brought you a gift," he said, disappearing outside. When he returned, he was holding a big golden cage with two sparrows perched inside. "These sparrows remind me of you—spunky and fun. They belong to you now."

"They are so cute," I squealed. "What a perfect gift."

I sat down next to K'inich Ajaw and gave him a kiss. Then, we started talking, and pretty soon, laughing and gossiping just like old times. It felt good to be home.

Everything is going to be just fine, I told myself. Yes, it was. I was certain of it.

The Green-Eyed Monster

For a while, K'inich Ajaw and I lived together without exchanging one angry word. He showed no more hints of the jealousy or possessiveness that had strained our marriage. I began to feel like myself again, a blend of the adventurous goddess who had once lived with her grandfather and the happy wife of a handsome god. I even resumed my friendship with Chac.

Chac hadn't changed one bit in the time we had not been friends. He still gleefully hurled lightning bolts down to earth and vigorously rattled the clouds with his thunder axe.

"No hard feelings?" he said when I first spotted him hanging around my house.

"Well, let's see," I said. "You killed me with your lightning bolt. Then you ditched me as a friend. Normally, that would be good reason to not like you anymore."

"Give me a break, Ixchel. I was only trying to save you from a bad fate," Chac explained. "Anyway, that's all in the past. Care to start over?"

"It's your lucky day, Chac!" I said, throwing my arms wide. "I am giving everyone a second chance. What do you have in mind for us today?"

"Want to throw some lightning bolts on the Mayan highlands?"

"Let's go," I agreed instantly and we sped off, just like old times.

Of course, I made sure I was home in time to prepare a meal for K'inich Ajaw. We ate black bean tamales in chili sauce together at dusk.

"What did you do today?" he asked.

"I helped Chac with his latest storm," I laughed. "He really is a character."

K'inich Ajaw frowned. "You know I've never liked him. He thinks he is such a hotshot with all those loud booms and crashes."

"You're right," I agreed. "But you can like him too, because even though he tries hard to be scary, he's really a goofball at heart."

"I don't find anything about him funny," replied K'inich Ajaw.

Clearly, it was time to change the subject. So I told K'inich Ajaw about how the sparrows chirped while I worked on my tapestry and how I had attended the births of fourteen healthy babies. Soon, it was my turn to bring light into the gathering darkness, so I kissed K'inich Ajaw and disappeared into the night.

After reuniting with Chac, I decided to spend more time with my grandfather, too. He seemed to have mellowed from when we shared a home.

"Ixchel," he cried when I showed up at his door. "I've been worried about you. I heard you went somewhere far way. I was hoping you would return soon, so I could see you again."

"I spent time in Meavan taking a break from K'inich Ajaw," I replied, hoping that Grandfather wouldn't question me further about the details. I knew he would only worry. When Grandfather started to worry, it always created more problems for me.

He looked at me long and hard. "Is everything really okay?" he asked. "Meavan is a long way to go to get away."

"I'm fine," I reassured him. "You were right. K'inich Ajaw has a temper. But we are working things out."

Grandfather nodded. "You always figure things out, even without my helpful advice," he teased.

I tried to steer our conversation in another direction to avoid any more questions.

"I have a case in the Middleworld that's been bothering me. There is a Mayan woman named Eme who's pregnant with her first child."

"Tell me all about her," said Grandfather. "Maybe I can help?"

"Eme has had a hard life. Her husband is a

difficult man. When he gets angry, he pushes Eme around. She's not very good at standing up for herself. Now, she's pregnant and praying to me every day to give her an easy childbirth."

"So, what's the problem?"

"The baby is going to have a difficult time coming into the world. He is sitting in the wrong position in his mother's womb. It will be a tricky birth. Eme and her baby will be at risk. I'm going to do all I can to ease her pain and make sure the baby is born healthy, but I am worried about how Eme will manage."

"Why?" asked Grandfather.

"Eme leaves tamales to burn in the fire and never feeds her dogs. They eat the scraps in her village. How can she care for a baby, especially after a difficult birth and with a bad husband?"

"Ixchel, people often change when they have responsibility thrust upon them. I think this woman will find a way to do what she needs to for her child. You may recall I once lived with a beautiful girl who did foolish things. She doesn't seem so foolish anymore."

Grandfather's compliment felt better than any gift of jewelry or jade. I blushed.

Grandfather was right. I had to trust that Eme would become a good mother. On my way home, still thinking about Eme, I almost ran head on into an old friend.

"Lost in thought? Care to share?" asked Chac Noh Ek.

"Chac Noh Ek," I squealed. "What have you been doing all this time?" I rushed into his arms and gave him a big kiss.

"Same old things. Signaling that it's time for war," he said with a grin. "Heard you were back though, so I came over to say hi."

"Thanks. It's good to be back. Now, don't you be a stranger. Come around and see me sometime, will you?"

"Do you think that's a good idea?" he asked, looking worried.

"Of course," I reassured him. "Your brother is a new man. We have an understanding. He trusts me and doesn't get so jealous anymore."

"Well, that's great news," said Chac Noh Ek. "I know he was miserable when you left. I hope he realizes what a lucky god he is to have you as his wife."

"You're so sweet, Chac Noh Ek. Promise you will come soon?" I asked. "I have some new tapestry designs I want to show you. K'inich Ajaw isn't too interested in that sort of thing."

"Sure," he said. "I would love to see your designs. But I have some Mayans who need my help right now, so I have to run."

"Okay," I said, wondering if Chac Noh Ek really believed me when I said K'inich Ajaw had changed. "I'll let you go only if you promise to come tomorrow," I said, grabbing him playfully by the arm.

"I'll try, Ixchel," he replied. "It's good to see you again." Then he sped off.

On the way home I thought about what I had said to Chac Noh Ek. Had K'inich Ajaw really changed? Was he no longer jealous? He didn't question me about how I spent my days, but he didn't seem very happy when I shared news that involved other gods. Lately, he had become more silent at dinner but claimed there was nothing wrong when I asked. I knew he was making a big effort to trust me, but I could tell it wasn't easy.

Then, I thought about my time with the Vulture King. He had always encouraged me to go out into the world and laughed along with me at my stories. He made me feel happy and unafraid. Problems like what to do with Eme would not have seemed so tricky to solve. I decided to talk about this with K'inich Ajaw. Better to clear the air to avoid any misunderstandings.

But my talk with K'inich Ajaw never happened. His mood just never seemed right. One day he came home very angry that Chac had upstaged him with a vicious storm. Another night, he was upset that the Mayans were making a big fuss over the corn god, K'awil.

"He's not that important," K'inich Ajaw muttered. "Mayans can survive without maize but not without the sun."

"Honestly, K'inich Ajaw," I said. "Everyone knows you're the boss, so why get so testy about it!"

"I'm not getting testy," grumbled K'inich Ajaw and stomped off.

Who can blame me for not bringing up my own personal issues? I had no idea how he would react.

What I started to do instead, was hang out a lot more with Chac, Grandfather, and Chac Noh Ek; anyone who was around and had time for some fun. I started to see less of K'inich Ajaw, and even when we did see one another, he was often in a bad mood. The times we laughed and gossiped began to fade into the past. Stubbornly, I continued to reassure myself that his black mood would pass.

I distracted myself by helping to brew storms with Chac and chatting with Chac Noh Ek.

Chac Noh Ek had interesting stories to tell. One day he saved a wounded warrior from a jaguar. The next day he rescued the same warrior and his troops from a swamp. These were just some of the perils of living in the Mayan world and why the Mayans relied so heavily on us to protect them.

A few nights later, I decided to share Chac Noh Ek's story with K'inich Ajaw, hoping to make him laugh. But, when I finished telling it with all the added embellishments I could think of, he just frowned.

"Why are you hanging out with my brother again?"

"What?" I said, wondering if I had heard him correctly.

This time, K'inich Ajaw practically spat at me. "I said, why are you hanging out with my brother again?" His voice was raised and his face was turning red.

"Why shouldn't I?" I responded.

K'inich Ajaw banged his fist on the table. "You know I don't like it when you see him."

"Since when do you get to tell me whom I can and can't see?" I shouted back. "Remember K'inich Ajaw, you don't get to boss me around. Remember the rules we discussed?"

K'inich Ajaw gave me a look that would have stopped a jaguar in its tracks. "Every day when I go out to light the world, I see you fooling around with someone else. First, it's Chac and his sidekick Kukulcan. Then, I saw you talking with K'awil the other day. What was that about?"

"It was nothing," I said. "We were just comparing our time in Xibalba. You know we both spent time there. I have every right to talk to anyone I choose."

I could not believe this. How had K'inich Ajaw come back to the same place I thought we had left far behind?

"What about all those things you promised me in the Vulture King's palace?" I demanded. "You said you would trust me. What happened to all those promises?"

"I'd keep my promises if you weren't so chummy with the other gods. It drives me crazy the way you act around them," he ranted, stamping his foot.

"How am I acting, K'inich Ajaw?" I shouted. "I'm just being myself, the girl you fell in love with."

I started to cry then. I was so overcome by anger and sadness that I dropped my head into my hands and moaned.

"Watch out, Ixchel, you're playing with fire!" K'inich Ajaw growled. Then, he stomped into our bedroom and slammed the door.

For the next few days, we avoided one another. When he was out, I stayed home to do my chores. When he came home in his black mood, I escaped quickly. Often I visited Grandfather, but

I never told him what was going on in my home.

But as you know, Grandfather has a sixth sense sometimes that things might not be what they seem.

"How is everything between you and K'inich Ajaw?" he asked one day out of the blue.

"We're fine," I blurted out too quickly.

"I have heard rumors," confided Grandfather. "Many of the gods say K'inich Ajaw looks ready to explode. The sun is shining too brightly these days. The Mayans are praying that their corn will not burn in the heat."

"I am sure K'inich Ajaw knows what he is doing," I replied. But in my heart I knew the signs from the beginning of our marriage, the dark moods, the false accusations, the banging of fists. A storm was brewing in my house and it didn't have anything to do with Chac.

"Grandfather, let me make you a tortilla with honey," I said hoping to change the subject.

That night, as I lit my moon torches and

placed them in their stone ring, I thought about the Mayans down below in the Middleworld. Eme was now caring for her healthy baby boy thanks to my intervention, while keeping her dogs fed and her tamales edible. The Mayans loved one another, tried to survive in a harsh world, and hoped for a safe passage to a new life after death. They counted on the gods in the Upperworld to help them make sense of their world. If I had the power to help them, surely I had the power to help myself.

What would be waiting for me when I got home? I was no longer sure. K'inich Ajaw and I had loved one another for so long, but lately all I felt was despair and sadness. Were we really meant to be a couple? You would think the sun and the moon belonged together, but we were more like two meteors on a collision course. The hope that filled me when I left the Vulture King's palace was fading. I wasn't sure about much anymore. What I did know was that I had already survived a lightning bolt, a trip to Xibalba, and being thrown out of Heaven. Whatever happened next, I knew I had the strength to pull through it. I also knew I could never be someone I was not. I could only just be me.

New Moon

For too long, I lived like someone perched on the edge of Lake Atilan. The lake itself is tranquil and the volcanoes that rim its edge are often quiet. It's possible to live there for a while, but not forever. Eventually, warning signs appear. Smoke wafts from a crater. Lava boils up to the surface. One day, a volcano erupts in an explosion of liquid rock. If you are standing too close, you'll get burned. If you don't run, you'll perish.

On the day that K'inich Ajaw exploded again, Chac whipped up a doozy of a storm. He made sure I could escape into the blackest of nights. K'inich Ajaw came searching, but he couldn't find me. I hid in a small cavity in a rock, where I wept silently. But things were different from the time K'inich Ajaw had cast me onto the banks of Lake Atilan.

This time, I decided to leave and I was never going back.

It took me an eternity to realize that K'inich Ajaw and I didn't really work well together. I have no regrets, though. I learned a lot through all the challenges I faced. Of course, Grandfather had been right. The universe was a dangerous place, but a goddess can't live in a cocoon forever. I wouldn't trade any of the experiences I had, even visiting Xibalba. At least I learned never to try to charm a demon.

Eventually, when I felt stronger, I came out of hiding. K'inich Ajaw showed up with his tail between his legs and tried to persuade me to return. I was determined to resist his honeyed words. He didn't give up easily, though. In fact, he's still trying. You know how stubborn he can be, and how persuasive. It makes me sad to see him, so I do whatever I can to avoid that. The Mayans say the moon is hiding when the sun is out, but I'm not hiding. I'm defining the boundary that separates us.

I have my own place in the Upperworld now. My moon ring is still close-by. Chac and Kukulcan moved it for me, so I didn't have to go anywhere near the home I once shared with K'inich Ajaw. But it's not as well placed as it once was on the hill—the Mayans say the moon does not shine as brightly as it used to and that K'inich Ajaw is responsible.

I've filled my house with more sparrows and painted my bedroom ceiling blue with yellow stars, just like my room in the Vulture King's palace. I think about him from time to time. I went back to visit Meavan once but it had been abandoned. I heard it was discovered by the outside world and bad things followed. I tried to find the Vulture King, but he had disappeared without a trace. However, he left me with a priceless gift. He made me realize I deserved to be myself. I would never again let someone else decide who I should be or how I should act. He showed me the power of unconditional love. If it were not for him, I might never have left my marriage.

I visit my grandfather often. I enjoy his company more now because he doesn't worry about me so much. Luckily, he never said "I told you so" after he found out what happened between K'inich Ajaw and me. He's as nosy as ever, but now, we usually end up laughing about something.

"The other day Chac started bragging about all the things he does for the Mayans," Grandfather told me.

"Oh no, I hate it when he does that."

"He got so puffed up, I had to say something to put him in his place."

"Like what?" I asked.

"I told him that being the moon goddess' grandfather outranked him."

"He must not have liked that!"

Grandfather smirked. "All he said was 'hmpff,' and stormed off."

"Grandfather, you are wicked. Why do you

egg him on and why are you always bragging about being my grandfather?"

"I'm proud of being your grandfather—even though it can be embarrassing!"

"How so?"

Grandfather had a twinkle in his eye. "Who wants to be associated with a goddess whose name means demon gas?"

"You know very well, Grandfather, that Ixchel means rainbow. I know the Mayans think rainbows are demon gas escaping from Xibalba, but I don't think they translate Ixchel that literally."

"Okay Demon Fart, if you say so!" he chortled.

"Grandfather!"

"How is Eme doing these days?" he asked to change the subject.

"She's doing really well and raising her son all by herself. He's turning out to be a responsible, hard-working boy."

"You see," said Grandfather. "I told you to have faith in her."

"Yes," I said. "You gave me good advice."

Grandfather looked at me and smiled. "I always do."

Where I Am Today

For centuries, I was the most powerful goddess in the Middleworld, or what today we call Mesoamerica. Mayan women would flock to my temples from far and wide. My survival as the wife of K'inich Ajaw inspired them. They admired the way I took charge of my own life and knew I would understand their pain and suffering. At least once in her lifetime, a woman would journey to my most important shrine on the island of Cozumel. Cozumel means "island of the sparrows" and is in the middle of the Caribbean Ocean, a twelve-mile canoe ride from the Mexican coast.

Women prayed to me to give them healthy babies, keep diseases away, and help them weave cotton into beautiful textiles. They also requested my help in providing them with well-matched and happy marriages. I took special care in answering these pleas. In exchange, women gave me cacao beans, jade stones, amber, turquoise, and feathered capes. Everyone knew how much I love to dress up!

As the modern world crept in and the Mayan way of life began to change, my influence among them waned. A new goddess, the Virgin Mary, became Our Mother Moon.

Today, my shrines are mostly in ruins; although, many women still visit them. Have I been forgotten? Not at all! I'm well known as the ancient goddess of love, healing, childbirth, and the moon. Women still pray to me for guidance. Not too long ago, Christiana Figueres, a leader in climate control policy, called me the Goddess of Reason, an inspiration for people to collaborate on ways to stop the world from getting any warmer. I wonder what K'inich Ajaw has to say about that?

There are plenty of places to see pictures of me today. The Mayans carved my image into stone, but over time, new artists have painted my portrait.

I have become a popular modern icon; so much so that resorts, healing centers, and a textile museum in Guatemala chose to name themselves after me. If there was a magazine of "pop" goddesses in Mesoamerica, I'm sure I would be on the cover. The picture I would choose would be of me as a beautiful goddess with long black hair and honey-colored skin that shimmers like the inside of an oyster shell. Of course, I would have a snake in my hair. It has become my signature accessory. That will never change.

Who Were the Ancient Mayans?

The ancient Mayans lived in Mesoamerica—in what is now the modern Mexican states of Yucatán, Quintana Roo, Campeche, Chiapas, and Tabasco and the modern nations of Guatemala, Belize, western Honduras, and El Salvador. Millions of their descendents still live in the same area, carrying on the traditions of their ancestors. However, in the last thirty years many Mayans have been forced to leave their native lands because of war and poverty. Today, thousands live in the United States.

The Mayan region accounted for one third of Mesoamerica; the region also included other cultures, the Olmec and the Aztec. The Mayan civilization developed through interaction with other Mesoamerican cultures.

Today there are hundreds of Mayan ruins scattered throughout Mexico, Guatemala, Belize, Honduras, and El Salvador. The well-preserved and popular sites are Palenque, Yaxchilán, Uxmal, and Chichén Itzá in Mexico, Tikal in Guatemala, and Copán in Honduras.

The Mayan ruins of Chichén Itzá.

Ruins of temples dedicated to Ixchel can be found on the islands of Cozumel and Mujeres, off of the coast of Cancun, Mexico.

Ruins on Cozumel.

133

What the Mayans Ate

The staple food of Mesoamerica was maize (corn), beans, and squashes. Most meals consisted of these three things.

Maize was used in many different ways. Maize flour was thinned with water and used to make drinks. *Atole*, a gruel drink was consumed twice a day, either hot or cold and flavored with chocolate, chili peppers, honey, squash seeds, or herbs. In death, Mayans were buried with a gourd of atole for their trip through Xibalba.

Maize flour was also made into dough, which was baked into tortillas or "little cakes."

The Mayans hunted game and birds, and fished for their meals. They ate venison, poultry, peccary (a pig-like animal), and dog. Crocodile, howler monkeys, armadillos, turtles, and iguanas were also sources of meat. Turtle and iguana eggs were prized. From the Caribbean, the Mayans harvested frogs, snails, and shellfish.

Meat was barbecued or roasted in a pit oven called a *pib*. The Mayans also boiled, steamed, smoked, or toasted their food over a hearth or in ceramic pots.

Cacao beans were one of the Mayans' most valuable crops. They were used to make chocolate drinks for the upper class and were also a form of currency, like money.

A cacao pod.

Honey was popular as a sweetener and came from bees that did not sting.

The Mayans produced alcoholic drinks by fermenting fruits. The two most popular alcoholic drinks were *balché*, made from the fermented bark of the balché tree and mixed with water and honey; and *chica*, made of fermented maize.

What the Mayans Wore

Stucco portrait head of Mayan male, 550–850 CE.

Mayan men pierced their ears, noses, and lips, while women pierced just their ears. Both men and women tattooed and painted their bodies. Teeth were filed into zigzag patterns and points and sometimes inlaid with jade.

Long hair was the style for both men and women. Men cut their hair short on either side and let some hair fall down their back in a braid decorated with feathers, or they wore elaborate headdresses. Women put their hair in braids, or created intricate hairstyles interwoven with cloth and feathers.

Men wore more jewelry than women did. Common adornments were bead collars; necklaces with pendants; and ornate earplugs that were so heavy they distorted men's earlobes.

Jade was highly valued and used as money. It was customary to fill a dead Mayan's mouth with jade beads, so the deceased would have money in the afterlife.

Mayan jade jewelry.

The Mayans wore loose-fitting clothes draped into cloaks or wrapped around their bodies in sarongs or skirts for women and kilts or loincloths for men. Women wore loose-fitting blouses or shifts called *huipils*.

Clothes were dyed in rich colors and adorned with hummingbird, macaw, and *quetzal* feathers. The most important people in the community wore puma, jaguar, and ocelot skin.

Though it might seem strange to us today, a sloping forehead and crossed eyes were both seen as marks of beauty, and were achieved with a lot of effort.

To create a sloping forehead, two boards were tied to the soft heads of newborns, one board against the forehead and another against the back of the head. After a few days, the boards were removed. The babies' heads would have been flattened—and stayed that way for a lifetime.

To create crossed eyes, a bead was tied to an infant's hair so that it dangled closely before him or her. This would eventually cause the child's eyes to turn inward.

On this page, Mayan huipils, belt, and skirt. Mid 20th century.

137

Playing Ball: *Pohatok*

The Ancient Mayan game of *pohatok* helped establish the foundation for modern ball games like soccer, football, basketball, and volleyball. But pohatok was not just played for entertainment and competition. In some cases, pohatok games ended in human sacrifice.

Powerful rulers would have war captives play ball against their captors. The outcome of the game was predetermined. The captives would be declared the losers and sacrificed to the gods—either by being decapitated or by having their hearts ripped out. (See the following section on human sacrifice.)

Ballcourt showing typical I-shape in Copán, Honduras.

Even normal games of pohatok were potentially life threatening. Players could be killed or seriously injured. The ball was made of heavy, solid rubber and could break bones. It was larger than a basketball. Sometimes an enemy captured in war might be bound up and used in place of the ball! The ballcourt came to symbolize the transition between life and death.

To protect themselves, pohatok players wore U-shaped belts or yokes, usually made of leather, rubber, or wood covered in quilted cotton. The yokes protected a player's ribs and hips. Knee pads and wrappings protected their arms and legs. Surprisingly, in striking contrast to all these practical measures, pohatok players often wore extremely elaborate headdresses.

Whistle in the shape of a ball player, 600–900 CE.

Most pohatok ballcourts were I-shaped with long, narrow playing alleys bordered by sloped, vertical, or stepped plastered walls painted in bright colors, and walled or open end zones at each end. The ballcourts varied greatly in size but the largest one, in the ancient city of Chichén Itzá, was 225 feet wide and 545 feet long—roughly twice the area of an American football field.

The rules of pohatok have been lost, but it is thought that players hit the ball back and forth using their hips, thighs, and upper arms, but not by kicking the ball or throwing it with their hands. Many ballcourts still retain two rings suspended vertically on opposing walls of the court. It is thought that these may have functioned as goals, although some researchers believe they were relatively late additions to the pohatok game.

Ballcourt in Chichén Itzá, Mexico. Note vertical rings protruding from walls.

Although pohatok was a game involving skill and chance, it was also acceptable for players to use trickery to increase their chances of winning. They say all's fair in love and war, and pohatok came pretty close to war!

In the *Popol Vuh*, the Mayan story of creation, pohatok is described as a contest between humans and the demons of Xibalba, and the ballcourt is the portal to the Underworld.

Without doubt, pohatok was an important part of Ancient Mayan life. Ballcourts were public spaces that were also used for other rituals, such as plays, musicals, and festivals. Musicians often performed at the games.

Close-up of ballcourt ring Chichén Itzá.

Ballcourt carving showing skull or demon in Chichén Itzá.

The Mayans and Human Sacrifice

In the Mayan creation story told in the Popol Vuh, the gods spilled their own blood onto maize to create the first humans. The Mayans believed that it was their duty to repay the gods with human blood. Blood was offered either through blood-letting (cutting yourself on purpose to draw blood) or through human sacrifice.

Kings and queens would cut themselves in public blood-letting ceremonies. These ceremonies allowed them to communicate with the gods, who helped them to make important decisions.

Sculpture depicting a sacred blood-letting sacrifice. King "Shield Jaguar" is shown holding a torch, while Queen "Lady Xoc" draws a barbed rope studded with obsidian blades through her tongue. It dates from around 725 CE.

The cheeks, ears, tongue, and penis were common parts of the body to pierce for blood-letting. Stingray spines, obsidian lancets, and carved bone awls were used to make the cuts.

The Mayans also offered humans as sacrifices to the gods. The Mayans believed this was essential to keeping order in the universe and maintaining the movement of the sun, moon, and stars. Without human sacrifices, the world would fall into chaos.

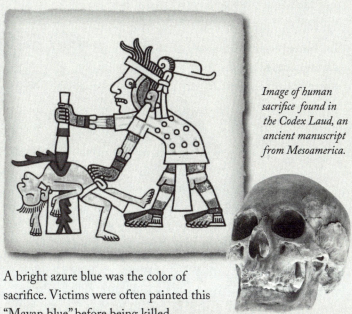

Image of human sacrifice found in the Codex Laud, an ancient manuscript from Mesoamerica.

A bright azure blue was the color of sacrifice. Victims were often painted this "Mayan blue" before being killed.

Who were the poor humans being sacrificed? Slaves, captives of war, criminals, and children—especially orphans—were the most frequent victims.

The Mayan Calendars

The Mayans used many calendars to record time: the *Haab'*, the *Sacred Round*, the *Calendar Round,* and the *Long Count.* The Mayans believed that time was cyclical—that the world was created, destroyed, and created again throughout time. If a particular day or period had a bad occurrence or misfortune, they believed this would recur when the same day returned in the future.

The Mayan solar calendar, the Haab', almost matched the length of one complete solar year. It had 365 days divided into eighteen months of twenty days each. Another five days were added at the end of the year to make a total of 365 days. Each of the months had its own name, like *Pop, Uo, Zip,* and *Tzec.*

The five extra days were called *Wayeb'* and considered an unlucky time of year. During this time, the Xibalban demons might travel to the Middleworld through caves to spread sickness, death, or decay. It was a time of great fear for the Mayans.

Another Mayan calendar was called the Sacred Round or *Tzolk'in*. Both the Tzolk'in and the Haab' worked independently but also together like interlocking cogwheels, creating another calendar known as the *Calendar Round*. A day in the Tzolk'in paired with another in the Haab' to create a day in the Calendar Round. It took fifty-two years before the combination of days repeated itself. This marked the end of one cycle and the beginning of another. The Mayans celebrated with a big festival.

The most famous Mayan calendar is called the Long Count. In this calendar, the Mayans counted days from the time the universe began on August 11, 3114 BCE. It is this calendar that gave rise to the rumor that the end of the world would fall on December 21, 2012. For the Mayans, this marked the end of one cycle, the Great Cycle, and the beginning of another.

A "Mayan calendar" now commonly sold to tourists.

Myth, Fact, or Fiction?

This is a novel based on ancient myths. Myths were never meant to be a fixed accounting. They were always open to reinterpretation and retelling. You might be interested to see how much of this telling was based on a skeleton of established myth, how much of it was made up or fictionalized, and how much of it was informed by research and facts.

The Rock Star of Heaven

Established Myth	Fact	Fiction
Ixchel lived with her grandfather in the Upperworld.		
Her grandfather guarded Ixchel closely.		Ixchel escaped her grandfather's surveillance to help Chac and Kukulcan whip up a storm.
		The Sun God, K'inich Ajaw, passed by and commented on Ixchel's hairdo.
Ixchel was beautiful, independent, and headstrong.		
		Ixchel lighted the night with torches she placed on a stone ring.

Love in Disguise

Established Myth	Fact	Fiction
K'inich Ajaw disguised himself as a hummingbird to win Ixchel's love.		
		Ixchel joined Ek Chuah, God of War, to watch warfare in the Middleworld.
	The Mayans only went to war if Chac Noh Ek, the Morning Star, was visible.	
Ixchel's grandfather grew jealous and shot the hummingbird with a blowgun.		
Ixchel fell in love with K'inich Ajaw while nursing the hummingbird back to health.		
K'inich Ajaw suggested they elope. Ixchel was reluctant at first but agreed.		

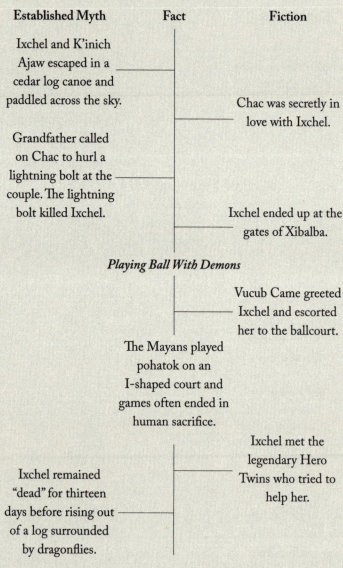

One Strike and You're Dead

Established Myth	Fact	Fiction
Ixchel and K'inich Ajaw escaped in a cedar log canoe and paddled across the sky.		
		Chac was secretly in love with Ixchel.
Grandfather called on Chac to hurl a lightning bolt at the couple. The lightning bolt killed Ixchel.		
		Ixchel ended up at the gates of Xibalba.

Playing Ball With Demons

	Fact	Fiction
		Vucub Came greeted Ixchel and escorted her to the ballcourt.
	The Mayans played pohatok on an I-shaped court and games often ended in human sacrifice.	
		Ixchel met the legendary Hero Twins who tried to help her.
Ixchel remained "dead" for thirteen days before rising out of a log surrounded by dragonflies.		

The Morning Star Comes Calling

Established Myth	Fact	Fiction
Ixchel and K'inich Ajaw got married. His brother, Chac Noh Ek, came to visit.		
	Mayan women believed Ixchel helped them with their weaving, and eased their pains when giving birth.	
K'inich Ajaw jealously accused Ixchel of encouraging his brother's visits.		
		K'inich Ajaw had Manik, God of Human Sacrifice, spy on Ixchel.
		Ixchel prepared a romantic dinner for K'inich Ajaw, intending to give him a gift.
In a fit of rage, K'inich Ajaw threw Ixchel out of the Upperworld and she landed on the banks of Lake Atilan.		

Under the Wing of a Vulture

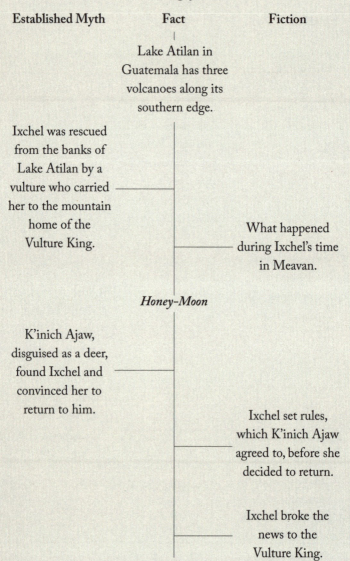

Established Myth	Fact	Fiction
	Lake Atilan in Guatemala has three volcanoes along its southern edge.	
Ixchel was rescued from the banks of Lake Atilan by a vulture who carried her to the mountain home of the Vulture King.		
		What happened during Ixchel's time in Meavan.

Honey-Moon

Established Myth	Fact	Fiction
K'inich Ajaw, disguised as a deer, found Ixchel and convinced her to return to him.		
		Ixchel set rules, which K'inich Ajaw agreed to, before she decided to return.
		Ixchel broke the news to the Vulture King.

The Green-Eyed Monster

Established Myth	Fact	Fiction
		Ixchel reconnected with Chac, Chac Noh Ek, and her grandfather.
		Ixchel wanted to help Eme and turned to her grandfather for advice.
K'inich Ajaw became jealous again, questioning Ixchel's relationship with Chac Noh Ek.		

New Moon

Established Myth	Fact	Fiction
In a jealous rage, K'inich Ajaw beat Ixchel so badly he destroyed her beauty.		
Through adversity, Ixchel grew stronger inside. She decided to leave K'inich Ajaw for good and escaped in the night.		

Established Myth	Fact	Fiction
	The Mayans believed that K'inich Ajaw's beating explained why the moon is not as bright as the sun and why the moon slips away when the sun arrives.	
		The new home Ixchel built for herself in the Upperworld.
		Ixchel's conversation with her grandfather.

END

Glossary

atole	Corn gruel
balché	Fermented drink made from soaking balché tree bark and roots in water and honey
copal	Tree resin used as incense
huipil	Mesoamerican blouse
kakaoh	A spicy chocolate drink
kanantabaa	"Take care of yourself"
pohatok	Mayan ball game
quetzal	Strikingly colored bird
sak'ha	A sweetened corn and honey gruel

Bibliography

Coe, Michael D. *The Maya.* Eighth Edition (Ancient People and Places). Thames & Hudson Inc., 2011.

Fisher, Leonard Everett. *Gods and Goddesses of the Ancient Maya.* Holiday House, 1990.

Foster, Lynn V. *Handbook to Life in the Ancient Maya World.* Oxford University Press, 2005.

Frankel, Valerie Estelle. *From Girl to Goddess—The Heroine's Journey through Myth and Legend.* McFarland and Company, 2000.

Galvin, Irene Flum. *The Ancient Maya (Cultures of the Past).* Benchmark Books, 1997.

McKillop, Heather. *The Ancient Maya: New Perspectives.* W. W. Norton & Company, 2006.

National Geographic Collector's Edition. *Mysteries of the MAYA: The Rise, Glory and Collapse of an Ancient Civilization.* Time Inc. Special Display, 2013.

Perl, Lila. *The Ancient Maya (People of the Ancient World).* Scholastic Library Publishing, 2005.

Schulman, Michael A. *Mayan and Aztec Mythology.* Enslow Publishers, 2001.

Stone, Merlin. *Ancient Mirrors of Womanhood (A Treasury of Goddess and Heroine Lore from Around the World).* Beacon Press, 1984, first published in 1979.

Taube, Karl. *Aztec & Maya Myths.* University of Texas Press, 1st edition, 1993.

Taube, Karl. *The Major Gods of Ancient Yucatan.* Dunbarton Oaks Research Library And Collection, 1997.

Tedlock, Dennis (Translator). *Popol Vuh: The Definitive Edition of the Mayan Book of the Dawn of Life and the Glories of Gods and Kings.* Touchstone: revised edition, 1996.

Whittington, E. Michael (Editor). *The Sport of Life and Death: The Mesoamerican Ballgame.* (Published in conjunction with the exhibition The Sport of Life and Death: The Mesoamerican Ballgame, organized by the Mint Museum of Art.) Thames & Hudson, 2001.